The Burning Light

THE
BURNING
LIGHT

BRADLEY P. BEAULIEU
AND ROB ZIEGLER

A TOM DOHERTY ASSOCIATES BOOK

NEW YORK

THE BURNING LIGHT

Copyright © 2016 by Bradley P. Beaulieu and Rob Ziegler

Cover art by Richard Anderson
Cover design by Christine Foltzer

Edited by Justin Landon

A Tor.com Book

Published by Tom Doherty Associates
175 Fifth Avenue
New York, NY 10010

www.tor.com

Tor® is a registered trademark of Macmillan Publishing Group, LLC.

ISBN 978-0-7653-9085-1 (ebook)
ISBN 978-0-7653-9086-8 (trade paperback)

First Edition: November 2016

The Burning Light

One

We Want the Vector

THREE MONTHS AGO...

THEY CAME TO THE first junkie at a landing maybe fifteen floors up. Matted hair hid her face; geologic layers of filth caked her skin. She sat cross-legged and blissed like some old ascetic on a mountain. She *stank*.

Solaas leveled his carbine at her. Goggins moved to grab her. The woman was oblivious.

She was tapped in, burning in the Light.

Colonel Melody Chu's mind reached out to her troops, her words an electric flicker of pure thought:

Don't even bother with her. She's just a junkie. We want the vector.

A column of bramble and vine grew up the stairwell to a hole in the roof, a pale coin of light far above. Chu and her Gov troops continued to spiral upward, up, up, up, sweating in mirror black graphene armor, lugging their electromag carbines. Four months here, and Chu knew this was what they would all remember. The Sisyphean grind of climbing these old towers, the saturating miasma of sewage rising off the canals below. New York was a ruin of shit and stairs.

My point is, Chu said as they climbed, *those old religions were on to something. I like sin. I like the idea of it.* They'd passed a street preacher outside the building, his little boat moored to the top of a light pole protruding a few inches above the canal's brown surface. In it he'd stood, bearded and wild. He'd gleamed with a wrath verging on joy, and ranted at them about Jesus. Jesus and salvation and Hell—his mind had reached out, briefly connecting, flashing images of crucifixion and fire. It had gotten Chu and her XO, Lieutenant Holder, talking.

Some of that God stuff's alright. Holder's mind leaned against Chu's, a perpetual offering, sharp as a blade and poised, awaiting her command. He was small, but solid, dedicated, the only one of her troops not raised in a Gov soldier collective. It was why Chu had chosen him. The others, their empathy had been groomed out of them—but not Holder. And empathy, Chu figured, was a useful compass, even if sometimes it got in the way. It was their mission to save people, after all . . .

Holder's words came as a shuffle of memory and thought as he followed her silently up the stairs. *There was a worship group up in the woods not far from my col-*

lective growing up. Mostly Amish, I think, but they'd thrown together pieces of the Koran and the Gita, too, and some of the other old books. Nice people. Weird, no doubt, tapped in to each other nonstop, feeding each other verses. No conversation even, just pure scripture. You'd run into them on the road or someplace and it'd be this biblical feedback loop. Crazy. Good folks, though, real decent, all about service and compassion, shit like that. Always helped us pull in our wheat. He reflected for a moment. *Made great cheese.*

I don't mean the stories, Chu told him, *Jesus and Allah and God. I don't care about God.*

A-fucking-men, chorused several of her troops, and dry chuckling broke their silence. Four months their minds had been connected. They'd begun to share the same sense of humor.

I'm talking about sin, Chu said. *Sin I get. Sin and repentance. Sin and salvation. Right and wrong. Consequences. Punishment.* Her mind opened to Holder and her troops. She let them feel her certainty, wrapped them into her personal memory of the street preacher—railing at them from the far side of a madness built of brimstone and visions of angels, but righteous, brimming with his cause, fierce.

Chu related to the man.

We are standing at the edge of the end of the world, she said.

She knew her reputation within the Gov collective. Captain Ahab Chu. She'd brought down whole collectives, and many of her superiors thought she was too quick on the trigger—especially after Latitude. When Latitude had come down, it had hit everyone where it hurt: in their balance sheets.

Obsessive. Precipitous decision making. These were the assessments made by functionaries higher up the food chain. After Latitude, Chu had presented her superiors a real problem. The abrupt extermination of six thousand people had struck them as . . . an overreaction. Yet no one could argue she wasn't effective.

They'd solved it by promoting her. After Latitude, they'd given her carte blanche to pursue the Light wherever it turned up—but with only a single squad: eleven washouts and Holder.

For her troops it was exile, far from the upriver promised land of cush overwatch postings in bloated finance and trade collectives, where the pay was good and the bribes were better. Exile, and her troops knew it. But Chu had won them over, cajoled them, harangued them, overpowered them with mission focus. She had personally stared into the Burning Light—and the Light had stared *back*. She knew it was coming. As they climbed the stairs, Chu let her troops feel it:

I have seen the Light! And the Light was no white

whale. It was a shark, a marauder. In her bones Chu knew this. And her troops, they were not outcasts. No, they were righteous. They were her crusaders. They gave her *Amens!*

Why's the Light got to chew on all these stankass junkies down here in New York? Solaas lamented. Chu felt his fatigue, heard his ragged breath echoing in the stairwell.

Moron, came Goggins, *it doesn't pick them because they're junkies. It* makes *them junkies.*

Yeah, well, it'd do my esprit de corps a shitload of good if it showed up once in a while in some posh Montreal whore collective.

Amen!

Goddamn.

I'd fight that fight.

If the Light showed up in a whorehouse, Solaas, Holder said, *we'd have to reassign you on ethical grounds.*

Why's that, Chief?

Gov doctrine specifically prohibits interfamilial combatants.

I don't get it.

Couldn't very well have you fighting your mother, now, could we.

You know my mother, Chief? A sly flicker played across Solaas's mind. *Are you my father?*

Fucking A right. and I'm gonna whup your ass, son, you

don't get up those stairs. Like sunlight off water, the joke reverberated among them, laughter playing across their minds, pushing the incessant churn and turn of the stairs to the background. Then it faded, the joke, the laughter, replaced again and always by the stink, by the grind, by the eternal climb.

That mean I get to call you Daddy?

Chu let herself smile.

~

They found the vector on the thirty-first floor. By some miracle the level hadn't been stripped by scavenger gangs. It was a maze of glass, steel, stained drywall, and rotted industrial carpet—a moment two centuries old frozen in time, unpeopled, caught in perpetual nightshift.

It was what passed as a security team that gave up the vector's position.

Goggins, on point, extended the spy eye, a black glass marble on his flat palm, beyond a blind corner. Its vision of the hallway beyond filled the minds of Chu and all her troops.

Well this is something new.

Through the spy eye, they all saw: four young bangers crouched around a lantern before an empty doorway. They were shirtless, tatted up with ink—not junkies themselves, just hired hands, hustlers getting paid for a night's work, AKs slung over shoulders or propped against the wall. Two played dice, the other two passed a joint back and forth. The apotheosis of readiness and discipline. Chu almost felt sorry for them.

We got the drop, Holder figured, *no problemo.*

Chu unbelted a flash disc, the size of an old silver dollar her father had shown her once. Her mind touched her troops, calm, emphatic.

Goggins. Solaas. High, low. Go on the flash. Professional groupings, nice and tight.

Chu rolled the disc down the hallway. Lightning flashed. Thunder pounded the air. Goggins and Solaas stepped around the corner, Goggins high, Solaas low. The *pock!-pock!-pock!-pock!* of hypersonic ceramic rounds scorching the air lasted less than a second.

Clear!

Chu stepped around the corner. Through a curl of white smoke she saw the bangers, all four of them shredded, utterly still.

Good work. Her mind leaned against Goggins and Solaas, laying on the positive vibes, like scratching two cats behind the ear.

The room beyond had once been a bathroom—robbed now of all its porcelain and stalls, just a hollow square with holes in the floors and walls where piping had been stripped. The vector sat there on the floor.

It isn't Zola, Chu observed. Holder gave her a look and she immediately regretted showing her disappointment.

No, Colonel Ahab, that is not your girl from Latitude. But a vector's a vector, correct?

Chu swallowed bitterness. *You are correct.*

Just a kid. Goggins knelt beside the vector as the troops gathered up. *Can't be older than nine.*

Goggins wasn't joking. The boy was barefoot, starved-looking in a stained T-shirt so big it reached his knees. Like the junkie they'd encountered below, he sat lotus, unaware of the troops standing over him, his mind deep in the Light. He was the anchor, the physical center around which the other junkies had arranged themselves in a sphere throughout the building. A halo, they called it. Through the vector, this kid, they connected to the Light.

Just a kid . . . , Goggins repeated, distantly this time, and Chu realized he was reaching out to the boy, testing his limits even as the boy was touching the Light.

Goggins! Filter up! Chu ordered. *We take no chances in this unit.*

Yeah, dipshit. Solaas slapped Goggins's shoulder, hard. *Don't get any on you, man.*

It was true. Chu knew from experience. The Light had touched her once. The memory wrapped her psyche like enflamed scar tissue. A memory she'd shared with her troops so they'd understand what they were fighting, and why.

Joy had been a kid too, like this boy. And like this boy she'd sat at the center, within a little paper-walled classroom. A spontaneous halo, they'd called it. Bodies lay all around her. Chu's teachers, friends, her parents. Gov troops who had come to the scene. Bodies, fallen over one another like fish dropped from a net. Dozens of them.

Her sister had surveyed the death, and her eyes had belonged to someone else, empty except for curiosity. When she'd seen Chu, standing stunned at the doorway, she'd smiled beatifically and lifted her hand, beckoning for Chu to come closer. And then the Light had reached out—

Chu drew the pistol from her hip.

Colonel! Holder reached out a hand to stay her, but not quick enough. Chu pressed the barrel against the kid's forehead as the memory washed over her. Moments ticked past. Her troops watched her. Her hand trembled.

The kid opened his eyes. He gazed up at Chu, the same empty-but-clear expression worn by ancient Buddhist statues. The same expression Chu's sister had worn. He smiled.

"I remember," he said. "I remember *you*." Chu felt it: the lighthouse strobe at the edge of her consciousness. It pulled her, grew brighter, tickling those places where she was most vulnerable, those places torn by loss.

A warm sensation rose up within her. The Light reached out, full of promise—

Chu raised the pistol and clubbed downward, hard and fast, clocking the kid across the temple. He went instantly limp. Chu holstered the pistol, then turned and walked away, her troops parting before her storm. For the first time in days, she spoke aloud.

"Bag the little fucker."

~

When Chu and her troops returned to canal level, junkies were still fleeing. They clambered into homemade canoes and kayaks, gondolas, old rowboats into which they'd jerry-rigged sails. They cast looks over their shoulders at the Gov troops; the fear in their eyes made Chu laugh.

Her troops ignored the junkies. Their boat, a sleek katana-class interceptor, was tied to an old flagpole protruding from the building's side. With its black diamond-plate decks and miniguns and electric props, it was like a barracuda here in the old city, a thing of startling wealth and ingenuity, of predatory speed. Goggins and Solaas hauled the vector aboard, stuffed into a black canvas bag, inside which he'd begun kicking.

Take him below, Chu told them. *Give him another injection. Make sure he's out.* In a day, maybe two, they'd give him to their contact a half-day up the Hudson, who in turn would pack him in a Gov transport and send him west, for Grandma and the scientists she kept in her employ.

The street preacher still stood in his little boat. He yelled at the sudden exodus of junkies, yelled at the emerging troops. He lived for moments like this, Chu was pretty sure, the transient illusion of a flock to shepherd.

You know what scares me? she asked Holder. They stood side by side against the katana's deck rail. *Every time I catch a glimpse, every time I feel the Light, it's just like when I was a girl, seeing it for the first time. I want to go in. I want to let it take me, just like it takes these fried-ass junkies. Even after everything we've seen, I still want it. How do you fight something that makes people want like that?* How did you fight sin?

For once, it had begun to rain. A wall of cool mist had boiled up out of the Atlantic and now it swept north, swallowing Manhattan's old square monoliths in a blanket of white.

I hate this city, Holder said finally, beads of mist clinging like mercury to his crewcut. He gazed up the canal, a canyon of vine-wrapped ruins. Chu followed his eyes to where larger, faster boats—boats with multiple sails and rows of oars—had appeared from around a corner a few blocks up. They'd begun to close on the fleeing junkies.

Labor traders.

They'd gather up the junkies and sell them off to the scavenger gangs, to whore shops, to black-market ship captains. The ones too weak for work, they'd dump overboard. Groups of these traders had begun tailing the katana: where Chu and her troops went, junkies fled like rats.

It's no wonder the Light shows up here, Holder said. *A single patrol for the whole city . . . how many halos you think are going on right now?*

The source says nine. But we won't reach any of them in time.

Exactly. We pop one, three more spring up in its place. We're rowing against the current here. Holder sucked his teeth. *Maybe Grandma can pull a string or two, get us some more troops?*

Grandma burned her bridges keeping me out of the stasis tanks after Latitude. She doesn't have any strings left to pull.

The oversight committee then?

They'd have to believe there's a credible threat. Chu gave Holder a look. *They haven't seen the Light.*

Up the block, grappling hooks flew. The Labor boats

began reeling in the smaller junkie boats. There was yelling. There were harpoons. There were guns. An idea occurred to Chu.

You say we need more patrols. You are definitely not wrong. She let the thought dangle like a rope between them, let Holder grab hold, pull it in. *And the Gov won't give them to us . . .*

Holder eyed her, skeptical at first, then nodding as he tasted the idea. His gaze went back to the Labor boats, and now he smiled. *We buy them.*

Chu nodded. *We buy them.*

Grandma's got chavos?

The one thing she does have.

Gentle precip scoured the shit smell from the air. It dimpled the canal with tiny silver rings. The street preacher, still railing, leveled a finger at Chu. She nodded to him, and smiled. His hand mimed a gun, aimed at her, and he winked: *bang!*, a moment of connection, as though this ruined city had just offered up in totem its strangest and most beautiful creature.

His sermon didn't miss a beat.

Chu turned her face up into the rain, and let herself be cleansed.

Two

I Never Regret You

ZOLA, BABY!

The call rang at the center of Zola's mind. Marco's touch, urgent, full of need, too long out of the Light. He had the itch. His presence in Zola's mind drew her forward, her gondola making slow progress up the canal. East 17th Street, a narrow canyon of concrete, dangling vines, the rusty press of anchored scavenger barges. Scrap vendors cried their wares, those last bits of sellable flesh picked from the bones of the old city. "Copper wire, yo! Hammered clean, real pure, no zinc! Take a look, mama!" "Porcelain, porcelain! Granite and marble! Whole tons, ya, barato real! Make me an offer!" Late summer humidity hung thick in the air; everything shimmered.

Zola!

Zola pressed her mind to Marco's: *Be there righteous fast, baby. We need food, ya. Then I'm home.* Home. Nowhere, everywhere. Wherever she was together with Marco. Wherever the Light called them.

She leaned hard on the oar, sweating, angling her gondola through a school of two-seater junks—a pack of Moby Jah boys whose faces turned and in unison showed Zola teeth filed into rows of incisors, sharklike and predatory. Their minds reached out for Zola's—a whisper, a collective unified by mad beats and fierce love for Moby Jah. They sailed around Zola's gondola, circles and figure eights, each rainbow-painted boat quick and moving in eerie coordination with the others, like the schools of mackerel skimming the concrete foundations below. They were *synced*. They turned their teeth at Zola and as they slid past, their minds couldn't quite touch hers and so they spoke aloud.

"Hot hot day, girl, ya. Be hot like you." Their words hung, an affront to the physical space between them and Zola. "Why your mind so far away, huh? You a junkie, girl? You are, ya. Junkie girl." Their laughter was the laughter of one, spilling from many, Moby Jah's laughter. "We take care of you, sweet junkie girl. Take care of you right." Out loud, their voices cut the air, made Zola's isolation burn, made her mind feel like a stone cast from a cliff, disconnected, alone. She bared her teeth and hissed at the men, and as she did a tremble worked itself out from somewhere deep in her body. The need to connect. Her hands shook. She fought the urge to vomit.

She had the itch, too.

"Junkie girl, all burned up." The Moby Jah boys corralled her. She regretted now coming at Stuy Town from the south. But Midtown was rife with thug cops hired by the Gov bitch whose sleek boat had prowled the city for months now, busting up halos. These cops, their sole focus was bagging junkies like Zola. She made to push through the Moby Jah boys, who'd cut her off now, their incisor smiles aimed her way. They toyed with her, steering their little boats at hers then veering away at the last instant—letting her know that if they wanted her, she was theirs. Zola reached into the chest pocket of her overalls, touched the tiny pearl-handled two-shot pistol she kept there. As she did, all the Moby Jah boys, every single one, snapped their heads to an electric barge up the way, crewed by three men and two women.

Cops.

Cops, with their little steel shields pinned to the chests of old Kevlar vests, pinned to the shoulders of torn T-shirts, pinned anywhere they couldn't be missed, as though the law had come down and baptized them of their sins and justified their natures. They'd all been slavers and thugs before the Gov bitch had come and bestowed badges. Now they were slavers and thugs who believed themselves legit.

Casually, the cops regarded the Moby Jah boys. They all held weapons—an old AK, pistols, a sawed-off. One old man held a simple fishing spear, a panting white bull terrier parked in his lap. The Moby Jah boys scattered, bobbing their heads twice to each stroke of the oar, and disappeared up an alley clogged with floating plastic.

It was just Zola then. She stood there in her gondola. The cops zeroed on her, all five of them. One of the men, a muscled blond who wore his badge pinned to a frayed straw hat, looked her up and down as the cop barge drew close. Zola braced herself to fight.

Zola, baby! Marco's mind, touching hers. *Need you here, girl. Soon, ya.*

Busy, baby. Hush.

"Ma'am," the blond cop said aloud, and touched the brim of his hat like some cowboy of yore as the two boats squeezed past each other in the narrow row between vendor barges. Zola forced herself to smile as gunwales nearly touched. She trembled, as much from fear now as from the itch. One of the cop women, big and scarred—she cocked her head back in contempt and said to the big blond:

"You ain't no super suave, Benji, you a lawman now. Act it, ya."

"Just being polite, Captain," and the blond smiled broadly at Zola. The woman called Captain, who wore old surplus camouflage with brass on the epaulets, and whose shoulders carried the exaggerated swagger of street authority—she pegged Zola with a narrow look.

"You look like someone maybe I know, girl. What's your name?" The boats, almost past each other now. Zola, still smiling, working the oar, trying to slip away—

The cop captain grabbed the gondola's gunwale. The woman's mind reached out, a probing flicker inside Zola's skull. Zola tried to project her own mind like a shield, press her thoughts to the captain's, the most natural of connections, a casual sharing of memory, the whispered merger of experience. She was Zola—once the star navigator at Latitude. She'd steered fleets of ships across the globe with her mind, easy as a smile, shared the simultaneous thoughts of ten thousand since her earliest memories. Connection had once been as natural as breathing. She pressed her thoughts forward, desperate now to connect with just one person.

There was nothing. The Light had burned her clean, and the captain knew it. Predatory recognition lit the woman's eyes.

"Junkie." She grinned horribly—brown wooden dentures, street-carved by some Rican whittler. "What's your name, junkie? Your name Zola? Got a friend wants to meet you. You're all she ever talks about." Zola, leaning hard on the oar, going nowhere. The captain held the gondola fast. The other cops scrambled, reaching for Zola, reaching for her boat. "Benji, get her," the captain ordered. Benji stepped across, ungainly, reaching.

Zola reacted—pure muscle memory, a fighting fitness class, part of her Latitude girlhood. Her foot snapped out, a straight kick that caught the big blond cop in the chest. His arms flailed. His eyes went wide. He fell back against the captain, then slid cursing between the two boats and into the canal. Zola brought her heel down on the captain's hand. The woman recoiled, hatred twisting her face. She lunged, but Zola was already on the gondola's oar, sliding slo-mo down the canal, just beyond reach, the vendors quiet now, old Carib mamas and Rican 'crete hawkers staring at the junkie girl heaving at the oar and the cops cursing in her wake and trying to get their barge turned around. It was too wide. It wedged itself across the canal. In the water, the blond cop sputtered, holding his hat high where it wouldn't get wet. The captain shook pain from her hand.

Zola, oaring away, faster now, the cop boat receding. She aimed her middle finger at the cop boat. "Chinga tu madre!"

The captain bared brown wooden teeth. She pulled a big pistol from a holster and brought it level.

"No!" The old man in the back of the cop barge stood, holding his fishing spear in one hand and the little white terrier in the other. "She's worth more alive."

"Still worth something dead."

"We know her now. We'll find her again."

Zola felt that pistol aiming for her head, but the shot never came. The captain didn't pull the trigger. Zola angled the gondola around a corner, a narrow alley, looked back, a last glimpse. The captain, sucking those teeth, her gun dangling at her side. The old man and the dog both looking Zola's way—the old man smiled at her.

$\sim$

Zola, baby! Marco, insistent now, full of possession and love and heat and fear. His thoughts reaching out like fingertips to touch Zola. For an instant they connected, a fluid rush of union, the way Zola used to do before the Light had burned the ability out of her. Now it only ever happened with Marco, a few days each time after they'd touched the Light together. *You good? Are you good?*

Ya. She wasn't caught, but maybe good was saying too much. There had been a time, before the Light, before Marco, when her life had been easy. Those memories, days in Latitude when she'd done what she'd been born to do—navigator, lover, collector of far-flung artifacts—it was as though that life had belonged to someone else. Now, with cops not far behind and Zola winding the gondola through random streets, trying to lose herself down alleys and blend into the press of boat traffic, she couldn't remember what it felt like to be something other than hunted. She worked the oar back and forth, let the air breathe against her sweat. *I'm good,* she told Marco, and then: *Baby, they know my name.*

Just a matter of time. But you're safe?

Safe.

Marco's relief flooded Zola. His mind braided through hers. Zola peered through his eyes—down the face of the Stuy tower from whose ruin he leaned, dangling from the dark cavity of an empty window, a vine clenched in one fist. Sunlight blazed off the East River far below, searing white light around which the city seemed insubstantial, a bardo of gray Stuy Town monoliths rising out of the spiraling foam of tidal vortices. Concrete and brine, a world of physical truths from which Zola felt Marco's mind recoil, the confines of what Jacirai called the mortal cage. Marco's thoughts bent wildly away from the moment, wrapped themselves instead around Zola's mind, zeroing playfully on the things he wanted to do to her—half fantasy, half memory. His lips on her neck, the gentle tug of his teeth on her nipples, the places his tongue would tease. But beneath those urges was a different, more desperate desire, a wish to be back among the folds of the Light, enveloped in a sea of thoughts so deep they'd never find the limits.

Into the Light . . . The whisper of a thought, unbidden, and Marco leaned far out the window, into blinding sun. Zola felt his fear, his urge to let go. *Don't make me wait, girl.*

He had the itch, bad.

Be easy, baby. Cops filling the day thick as mosquitoes. But I'm coming, ya. Soon now. Zola's shoulders flexed against the oar; she fought the shake in her hands. *Real soon, baby.*

She worked the gondola through the boat traffic—the scavenger barges loaded down with rebar, 'crete dust, and steel girders stripped from uptown scrapers and towed by Rican men in longboats, oars like centipede legs sculling the canal; the schools of rainbow junks, men shirtless in the heat, on the prowl for a hustle, their shaved heads dark and nodding in unison to the beats of Moby Jah; black market banker types who rode in the posh leather seats of gleaming polymer-hulled boats, their collars buttoned priest-high and bound by silk cravats, faces vacant, meditative: their minds riding the ebb and flow of currency from one black account to another.

Through the traffic, back onto East 17th now, a wide deep pool at the intersection of First Ave. Old Rican mommas had set up shop there, rafting square garden barges together in the afternoon sun. They sat, wrapped in the personal shade of thin shawls, behind tables stacked with jars of herbs and spice seeds. From behind giant aviator shades, they watched as East Siders browsed their garden rows.

Zola scanned the avenue for cops, and saw none. She felt exposed: this was a place where normal people shopped—as normal as people in this city got. These new cops, they gave rewards for junkies. But junkies had needs too. Marco had needs.

Zola steeled herself, thrust her chin defiantly forward, and threw a line. She stepped out into a bed of root vegetables. This she wandered slowly, probing bare toes into black topsoil disturbed by a thousand shoppers before her—skinny carrots, onions whose impressive stalks belied bulbs no bigger than her thumb. The tomatoes, however, were real beauties. They hung pendulous, oxhearts nearly too heavy for their vines, on the yellow side, not quite ripe. Perfect. Bending low, Zola reached out to touch one. In the corner of her mind, she felt the pressure of Marco's need, his itch. It made her hand shake.

"¿Puedo ayudarte, hija?" A Rican woman stepped toward her. In her insectoid shades, the distorted reflection of Zola's gaunt face. Zola picked two tomatoes and held them up.

"This. Saw palmetto, too. And mullein. I need it dry, madre. Dry enough to burn, ya."

The Rican woman said nothing. With a finger she

pushed the shades up over her brow—her black eyes fixed on the tomatoes, clocked the tremor in Zola's hand. A stillness came over her and she stood like that, poised, hand raised in mid-gesture, occupied by the sort of silence that meant her mind had merged with others from her collective. For a beat, it was like time stopping, then the madre's eyes refocused on Zola. Her expression was hard.

"East Side Growers don't want no junkies in our gardens. You got to go, honey." She glanced pointedly down the row, where a young, East Side mother leaned over, inspecting a patch of leeks. A clean skirt and hair pulled back and rings on her fingers, the moneyed ease of someone who had never seen bad shit—or, Zola figured, the Burning Light of Truth. Beside the woman sat a toddler in denim overalls, the miniature, clean version of what Zola wore. Desirable customers. The Rican woman waved a hand as though Zola were a fly to be shooed. "You got to go!"

"Junkies got to eat, too, madre." Zola held up the tomatoes. "Already picked them, ya. Got to buy them now."

The madre eyed Zola for another hard beat. Then, sucking her lip, she jerked her head forward, dropping the shades to her nose. She aimed a finger at the ground, as though some immutable principle lay etched there in the garden's topsoil.

"Chavos," she stated.

"Si, si." Zola clutched the front of her overalls and shook them. Coins jingled in the bib pocket.

"No. Chavos real." The madre raised an index finger to her temple. She went still again, and this time Zola felt the whisper of the woman's mind reaching out, to Zola this time, trying to connect, the way the cop woman's had—but in Zola's lobes, atrophied by the breadths and depths to which the Light had taken her, it was almost intangible, as impossible to touch as smoke. When she'd come to the old city from Latitude, Zola had still been able to connect. She could've reached out and joined the madre, traded real currency. The Light, though, took its tithe. After three trips with Marco and the others, it was hard to connect. After ten, Zola could only connect in the calm days that followed each trip. After twenty, her hands had begun to shake and her dreams had turned to white fire, and now she couldn't join anyone anymore, except for Marco. Jacirai said it might come back if she stopped, but Zola doubted it. It was a sacrifice they all made, those who wanted to touch the Light. Sometimes it seemed too much.

"Real is real, ya." Zola shook the coins again. "I pay, madre, you sell."

The shakes set in again, deep in Zola's chest, emanating out to her limbs. The itch, the need to connect.

Out on the canal, the cop boat appeared, sailing east now. Under her breath, Zola cursed. She turned away from the cops, held a hand to her brow to obscure her face. The Rican woman watched, her gaze switching from Zola to the cops and back, clocking the whole thing. She pursed her lips, considering.

"Please, madre," Zola pleaded. "I see it in your face you think I got no life worth living, ya. But I got love, and someone to live for, someone who loves me. Those puto slave cops take me," a glance toward the cop boat, "and that's all gone. I'll be gone. Please." The madre frowned, not without sympathy.

"You take them." Indicating the tomatoes. "You take them and you go."

Heat worked its way up Zola's spine. Marco's mind, itching bad.

Zola, baby . . . Leaning far out into the light, yearning to let go. Zola stepped closer to the Rican woman.

"And saw palmetto," she insisted. "Mullein, too. I need it real dry, ya. Dry enough to burn." Her whole body afire with the itch, her reflection twisting in the woman's shades. "Thank you, madre."

~

"You got to be careful, baby." Marco, framed in pale light

at the open edge of the thirty-fifth floor, where once had been floor-to-ceiling windows and now hung a thick screen of vines. He sat naked, arms wrapped around his knees, the immediacy of his voice a source of grounding warmth in the building's gutted solitude. "That defiance of yours get you killed, ya." He meant the cops. He'd been there with Zola, watching through her eyes, listening through her ears. He'd seen the woman cop raise her pistol.

"It's okay," Zola told him. She'd built a small driftwood fire on bare concrete near the edge where its smoke would leak out into the day, and now cut tomatoes into palm-thick slices with the same folding knife she used for cleaning fish. It was an old residential building. Rican and Carib scavs had stripped it long ago, like most of the old city core, mined it for raw materials for the new cities up north along the Hudson. Nothing remained now but concrete struts, spines of rebar—Stuy Town a Venetian ruin rising from the river far below.

Marco had tried to make good on his promises, had come on determined and rough, kissing, groping. But he had the itch bad and couldn't get it up. After, they had lain there in cavernous isolation, wrapped in the coarse folds of an ancient army surplus blanket. Zola had tried to hold him.

"Lo siento, baby," he'd said, and turned away.

She'd run her fingertips over the tattoos on his shoulders and along his arms, images he'd designed himself, a narrative tapestry of his short life, all the places he'd ever been, inked into his skin. A painted kabuki mask on his shoulder, emblemizing his time in a Tokyo farming arcology. A spiraling, fanged snake he'd had done in a Sao Paolo art collective. An AK over his heart, from Mexico City. The two of them had connected in the Light, gone deep into each other's memories. He was rough and uneducated, at least in the ways Zola was educated, but the breadth of his experience made her feel small, and she liked that. He'd been everywhere. He'd sought vivid experiences, his true north the ardent belief in a life wholly lived, equating meaning to the most raw sensations. He hungered to find the limits of his being. It was only natural he would come to the Burning Light.

During the cool nights between the ritual halos when the itch kept them from sleeping, Zola would lay an index finger against his skin, and in the low firelight whatever image she touched, Marco would tell that story—not like people did now, but with words, spinning a tale like people used to do. Zola would recall his memory, a memory now her own. She loved these stories, these memories he'd given her—always exotic, far-flung, full of fighting and broken, drunken hearts. With each one a piece of Marco would fall into place, some historical marker helping to map him; his smile, his dark moods, each shared memory a stepping stone, bringing him closer to Zola.

There in the cavernous twilight of the empty Stuy tower, they lay together in strained silence. His failure frightened them. It marked his decline.

"We should go somewhere," Zola'd said into the growing darkness. "Make a new tattoo."

For a long while, they both simply breathed, relishing that sweet lie.

"All times are now, ya," Marco said finally, maybe to Zola or maybe only to himself, and then he'd slipped from under the blanket and away from her. *All times are now.* It was a meaningless phrase to Zola, the sort of thing Jacirai would declare in one of his mad sermons between rituals, the Burning Lighters stationed in a sphere around him in whatever vacant tower they squatted. His eyes would roll back so only the whites were visible and he would growl and spit and give utterance like some feral demon—from on high, ya, the echoes of things they'd all touched in the Light. His sermons, sometimes they spoke straight to the heart of truth—that in the Light they all became something more, godlike in the depth of their union—and sometimes it seemed all nonsense, just noise to keep everyone going, feeling connected until the next ritual, the next sweet burn.

As Zola covered the tomato slices in an herb mixture—thyme, basil, sea salt, and white pepper, which she took in pinches from a small leather pouch—she watched Marco. He looked small, boyish. Ribs etched his back, and he trembled. It was as though the Light had hollowed him, as though he were receding in stages from his own flesh so that others might touch the truth. Thus was his lot, a medium for the Light. Zola strained to touch her mind to his, and for a moment they reveled in closeness.

You give so much.

She set the tomatoes to fry in a small pan on the fire, turning them every so often with the tip of her knife. The sun had half set and turned the water below the color of blood. Zola figured there was something natural in this space, in moments like this, something primitive and true. Wrapped in the blanket, she imagined herself like the Anasazi, staring out at the desert from the high safety of their hollow cliffs. She'd had a collection of Anasazi relics once, in a special plexi case in her Latitude abode. Pot shards with zigzag designs, a stone grinding tool. Prizes in her collection of souvenirs from all over the globe, talismans to the idea of a world growing smaller, coming together, like it had been when the old cities had been filled with people instead of water—but now that was all gone. The sun turned red over the canals and flooded brownstones, a different sort of desert. Down there, the cops hunted junkies. And those cops knew Zola's name.

"Baby. Eat." She held the pan and beckoned Marco to the fire. He smiled weakly.

"Lo siento, baby, I just got no appetite. Looks mad tasty, ya, but . . ." He dropped his face into his hands and squeezed his forehead. "My head, killing me fucking bad."

The Rican madre had given Zola the mullein and saw palmetto wrapped in two big banana leaves, and these Zola pulled from the pocket of her discarded overalls. She mixed the herbs together with some local rooftop dirt weed and tobacco from a stale cigarette, both of which she'd kept hidden in a little wooden box in her day bag. She rolled it all together in a tear of notebook paper and licked it shut.

"You ever regret it?" Marco asked, his face still cradled in his palms. Zola leaned close into the fire to light the joint. Marco looked at her. "*Do* you?" His face hollow, an apparition of who he'd once been. A stab of fear shot through Zola: Marco was fading, and they both knew it. Zola understood exactly what he was asking. Did she regret losing that other life? Was the Light worth the sacrifice? Was *he* worth it?

That other life. Even the memory of it felt somehow

false, a life so wholly different it might never have been.

~

Her navigator's abode. A slice of sky wrapped in photosensitive plexi, the sunlight pouring in. This was what Zola remembered. Resting in the deep folds of an African leather sofa, bathing in sunlight as she did the work for which she was born. Navigating. Reaching out to her ships, their eager minds meeting hers as they cut across some far-flung stretch of globe. Around Zola, her collection of artifacts. Zulu spears and Siberian oak tables, pottery shards and computer keyboards, ornamental wristwatches and Amazonian fertility totems, all arranged geographically, a ritual layout of lost histories. Curled up at her feet, two great and friendly wolfhounds.

Her ships, sunlight in the mornings. Latitude filling her mind, that easy hive hum. Six thousand people living their lives, their minds shared with hers. The sensate minutiae of their mornings, breakfast smells and first-light trysts, people doing Latitude's work. The hum, a greater metabolism in which Zola had always been immersed, whose unifying thread was a collective will bent on the flow of goods, the accumulation and reinvestment of boggling amounts of currency. Connection. This was what she remembered.

And Byron. His dense physicality, the gentle way his mind braided through hers. Her primary, her mate. Born the same day, the two of them. Brought forth from the laboratory wombs deep in the Latitude vaults. Connection—this was what they were designed for. Brought forth together, the two of them, already immersed in the buzz of Latitude's collective ebb and flow. The cinnamon and musk smell of him, his eyes lighting up when it was impossible to tell whose thought belonged to whom, his thick arm splayed possessively across her in sleep. Born together, born for each other.

She knew now that the Light had touched her first in dreams. Now she could recognize it. Half-remembered images, how she'd start awake, and the aftereffects, a manic residue she carried through her days. In sleep, the Light came to her as quick, stabbing visions. The ocean's slate horizon—out there, beyond the globe's long curve, a flash, brighter than the sun. Pure white light.

She'd wake next to Byron in a sweating tangle of Milanese silk, the morning sun slashing horizontally across the apartment, the dream already fading. Beside her, Byron would sleep on, the bulk of him rising and falling with meaty breaths, gentle and oblivious, his dreams the dreams of Latitude. A flash. That was all it had been, just a dream.

But then the Light came to her when she was awake.

Her abode was on the thirteenth floor of Latitude's North River Tower, a diamond of steel and plexi that rose like a rapier tip from the bank of the Hudson. A monument to the rebirth of global trade. Latitude, reaching out, touching every part of the world, making it smaller every year. One day, it would be the way it had been centuries before, cheap goods from across the world filling everyone's life. This was Latitude's directive, and it was therefore Zola's. Deep in the nest of an African leather sofa, she worked with her face turned up to the morning sun.

Four thousand miles away, a fleet of ten catties sailed in formation, parallel to a thin white ribbon of sand just visible against the eastern horizon. These were her ships, a day out of Ivory Coast, loaded up with industrial diamonds, copper, manganese, gunning for the North Atlantic. Their sails dug hard into wind blown from a storm to the south. Their minds pressed Zola's, full of the joy of their sprint.

She ran them north, and as she did Byron emerged naked from sleep and came to her, rubbing sleep from his soft moon face. Zola pulled him down and straddled him, and rode him in the sofa's smooth leather as the sun warmed them both. She let the ships feel him, let *him* feel the ships and salt air and motion. Together they watched the prows slice long swells into rainbows of silver spray. They felt the waves, their endless roll perfectly in tune with Zola's movements. In the freedom of it he laughed and bit Zola's neck, and through it all Latitude was there, in the background, encouraging, other minds reaching out, joining them in the moment. Light filled the abode and the white orb of the sun seemed to grow around them, and somehow *inside* Zola, too, a hot coin at the top of her spine, spreading, like she was falling into it—

I AM.

The statement blotted out everything. It wasn't a voice, or even thought. It was simply knowledge.

I AM.

Some axis tilted inside Zola, gravity changed direction. The dream returned to her. That lighthouse flash. Now there were people on a shoreline—they stared at the horizon. They had been there for a long time, she sensed, watching. All at once they turned. Fire filled their eyes.

I KNOW YOU.

It was her face. All of them, they were *her*.

YOU ARE.

White light seared the horizon. It grew, a star exploding, an infant taking its first breath. It enveloped the sea, the shoreline, the people. White fire, a magnesium flare, the hot spot in her head exploding, filling her, and everything else was gone.

When the Light receded, Zola didn't know how much time had passed. There on the couch, blinking, still atop Byron; her heart hammered in her ears. Her mind reached out to her ships. They were disconcerted, still running north, but slow now, their formation faltering. Byron, one hand frozen against her breast, gaped at Zola.

"I am . . . ," he said after a moment, "*amazing.*"

"Did you . . . ?" Zola, struggling to reel in her ships, didn't know what to say. *Did you see . . . ?*

You shone like the SUN, girl.

No. The light. Come on, did you see it?

Byron, grinning . . . *I saw.*

~

High up in the dead Stuy tower, Zola stared into the fire and exhaled smoke. "Sometimes I regret, ya." Honest, because she always was with Marco. "I miss my ships."

The itch came on strong and for a moment it made Zola shudder under her blanket. Some days, like today, when it had been a long time between ceremonies, it felt as though her soul had been stretched between two faraway moments in time. It felt like it might snap. Her mind railed against its isolation.

"I regret it bad, sometimes. Wish I could unsee everything the Light shown me. Just wake up one morning back in Latitude, my people all around, and me linked with my fleet of big catties. Sailing down the North Sea, steering them home. I miss my people." The white noise press of Latitude's minds, gentle as low surf breaking. All of them dead now, all of it gone. She said, "Latitude collected our memories. I never knew anything but that, like time just washed through us and collected in a pool. Never lost. Now it's like it never happened." Outside, the city had gone red as the sun bled away. "I lose every moment, like I'm not even here, ya. The time's just gone, no proof I ever witnessed it."

"The Light reach out to you long before I ever met you," Marco said. With his feet at the edge of the drop, he shivered. "You a medium, same as me. Why that Gov lady got such a thing for you—she knows it." He looked at Zola. "When I'm gone, you got to step in, answer the call."

"Don't talk like that. You going nowhere." Zola rose from the fire and moved to Marco. She sat behind him, wrapped herself and the blanket around him, meeting as much of his skin with hers as she could. He was cold. "This'll help your head, baby." Motherly, she wedged the joint between his lips.

He sucked deep. As he held the smoke in his lungs

Zola could feel his heart stutter against her breast. His tremble eased then, and Zola pressed her lips to his back, to his neck, to his shoulder. Her mind reached out for his, but she didn't have enough left, and neither did he. They both needed to touch the Light. From within the isolation of her own skull, she whispered in his ear:

"I never regret you."

Three

The Source Doesn't Miss

GOT SOME MEAT FOR YOU. The woman cop stood like a Kevlared George Washington in the bow of a labor boat with too many makeshift canvas sails, her shotgun propped over one shoulder and her chin cocked back, portrait-ready. Her crew heaved-to and readied lines. *One kicking, one dead.*

Watching her from the deck of the katana, Chu and Holder exchanged a sour glance. A shared prayer to whatever gods punished vainglory.

Please dump her overboard.

They'd dealt with this woman before. Like all the new cops, she was a hustler. Figured it was her place to scam and dicker. She was arrogant—she'd sewn stars onto the breast of her faded surplus fatigues and taken to calling herself Captain. Chu eyed her coolly. The katana's gunwales bristled with miniguns, their aim aligned with Chu's mood, which right now was an inclination to turn Captain's boat into a steaming cavity in the water. Her mind met Captain's:

Good for you. Gender?

One male, dead one's a bitch. The woman's mind, whenever it touched Chu's, felt like cruel laughter and broken glass. Holder in particular bristled whenever the woman came around. He tried to hide it, but Chu saw: Captain offended his sense of decency. The raw sweat stink rolling off her and her crew, the sun-blistered skin of her cheeks, the rust along her big shotgun's barrel. Thugs, every single one of these paid cops. Downtown water rats, slavers. Wild born, raised in the holds of scavenger barges or low in the old tower cores, those dark and half-submerged bazaars where people trafficked in pure labor, a vulture economy that revolved around scraping clean the corpse of the old world. Thugs, to whom Chu had given badges, specifically for their expertise in human bondage. Holder stood there, glaring.

"He ain't so friendly," commented Captain's second in command, the muscled blond. He eyed Holder.

"Oh, I'm friendly," Holder said, also aloud, "it's just the *reek* down here. The canal stink. Rats crawling all over one another. Makes my skin itch." The two men pointed humorless smiles at each other.

Captain's mind reached out and for an instant Chu caught a glimpse of herself through the woman's eyes: face impassive, stars pinned to epaulets—real stars, forged of dedicated service and sacrifice, not cheap bits of brass found in some previous century's abandoned surplus depot.

Let's see what you've got, Chu demanded. Captain's crew hoisted two bundles, bound in tarps and rope, from the labor boat's hull. These they heaved onto the katana's deck. Chu pulled a blade, stepped forward, cut one of the bundles open.

A girl, or at least what *had* been a girl. Maybe fifteen years old, face cratered around a large-caliber bullet hole beneath one eye. Chu frowned.

Not the one I'm looking for.

She the one we found. Up Stuy way, just like you said, Colonel Mama. Mama: the one with the purse, the one who doled out coins and candy.

The vector I'm looking for is older. Twenty-five or so.

Don't care if this girl one and the same with the one you got a taste for. That—Captain indicated the corpse with the barrel of her shotgun—*still a medium, and mediums what we get paid to get. We get, you pay, that's the deal. No doubt what she is, found her doing ritual, bunch of junkies up in the old towers. Righteous trash, straight firing their brains, and she at the heart of it, zactly way you said.* Captain showed teeth—wooden dentures rotted brown. *Don't know where you get your info, Mama, but we never come up zactly empty.*

My source doesn't miss. Chu gestured at the other bundle. *What about that one?*

We pump him full of tranq, but he come around soon enough. He rascally, though. Sneaky little fuck, you watch out.

Chu cut rope and canvas with her blade. The bundle spilled open. An old man this time, a slit of white barely visible beneath still eyelids. A finger to the neck: Chu felt a pulse.

Was he touching the Light when you caught him?

No, but enough people said. He a straight fire priest, for sure, Mama.

"For sure," echoed the big blond.

You don't want him, we take him along with us, find some use for him. Captain leered, her look ever hungry. *Got flesh on him before his fingers show bone, a measure of good hard work left there, straight cash for us, no doubt.*

"No doubt." Again the blond ape with the hat and the AK smiled.

The bundle on the deck stirred; the old man's eyes fluttered open, seemed to register nothing, until they fixed on Chu. Then they went wide with fear. Chu pressed her mind to the old man's, felt scorched pathways, the memory of white light, profound union. Grief now at his own isolation.

Chu gestured. Goggins and Solaas stepped forward.

In the sun, their graphene armor gleamed. The old man moaned as they hauled him out of the bundle and up to his feet. His mouth hung open and he gave Chu a pleading look, but only vowels emerged. Goggins and Solaas dragged him away, down to the hold below. If he was a vector, Grandma could use him.

You get your pay. Chu's mind touched Captain's. Currency flowed. Captain smiled big wet dentures. Chu jerked her chin at the corpse. *You can hang on to that. Keep yourself ready down around Stuy Town. I'll update you when my source gives me new vectors. Any more you bring me, you know I'll pay.*

Captain slung her shotgun over a shoulder and hoisted the body. Chu considered the corpse, propped there for an instant on the gunwale before it dropped over the side and into the rancid river.

If you come across the one I want, Captain, don't kill her. Don't try to take her. Reach me instead. I'll come for her myself.

A strange stillness came over Captain and her crew. She exchanged a glance with the skinny old man to her left, who wore a wide-brimmed straw hat and held a little terrier on his lap. Sucking sounds came from her dentures as she gave Chu a sly look.

You still pay, though.

If your information leads me to Zola, specifically to her . . . I pay triple.

We maybe seen her then.

Where? What happened?

Up Stuy way, where we got the others. We got righteous eyes on her, up close and personal. She was pushing a boat down the street. Captain shrugged. *She got loose.*

It happens, the cowboy blond said.

Colonel Chu swallowed fury. They floated in a swath of open water, two cop boats lashed together, one of them a slaver, the other clearly military—traffic gave them a wide berth. The shit and oil stink of the East River cloyed at Chu's nostrils; the towers of the old scrapers rose along either bank, flooded, hollow, dead. For an instant, her hatred for this city was so intense she thought she would burst into flame. She wanted to burn the whole place down with her.

Why you got such a bone for one girl, hey? Captain wondered.

Chu considered her answers, her thoughts drifting to her source, the woman strapped to the table in the hold below. *She was the one who got away,* she said after a moment, and for some reason this made Captain smile. *I know Zola's in Stuy Town. Get eyes on her again.*

For sure, Colonel Mama. Girl's as good as got.

So you say. Now get off my boat. You stink.

⁓

"You were wrong." Chu reversed a small steel chair and sat straddling it, arms folded across the back, facing the restraining table. A stale circle of daylight fell through a tiny round portal high on one wall, and in this the woman on the table stared at the ceiling, wordless. She had long ago ceased to struggle against the straps. Speaking aloud, Chu pressed. "They missed her."

The woman let out a long breath and turned her head to look at Chu. Sweat beaded the woman's forehead; her neck pulsed slightly where a tube entered it, attached to a fat IV bag slung overhead. Chu swallowed hard. It fazed her, every time. The woman, staring. In the sunken cheeks, in the delicate brow, Chu still saw the child she had been. Her face identical to Chu's own, but underfed, junkie-glazed. A distorted mirror, a version of self that had traveled a twisted path, but one near enough to Chu's own it felt close enough to touch, close enough it could contaminate.

"They miss her every time," Chu said.

The source stared, trying to connect—but Chu had filtered herself, lest the source's mind touch hers; lest she bring in the Light. Chu waited, impassive, until finally the woman seemed to collapse in on herself, a long release of breath, resignation. She spoke aloud.

"I see it in your face," she said. "You try to keep it hidden, but I can tell. This hurts you, sister," and she smiled.

Sister: the word laid out between them, an indictment, charting cold years of bondage.

Chu breathed, measured and deep, slowing her heart rate. She spoke through clenched teeth. "I need you to see vectors." Vectors—not fire priests, not blazers or burners or Lighters, and especially not the superstition-laden "medium." Vectors, as in for disease.

"I do see them," the woman on the table said. "All of them. Whenever they touch the Light. But I never see the girl you want. Zola. Never on her own, only glimpses of her through the eyes of others. What does that tell you?"

"She *is* a vector," Chu insisted. "And she's important. The Light reached all the way into Latitude for her. It wants her."

"What you want me to see isn't what's there. What can I do—"

Chu's hand slammed down on the table. The source's eyes lit with animal fear. It made Chu's heart clench. She withdrew her hand. When she spoke, her voice was calm.

"See better."

"The Light wants what it wants. It wants to awaken. Maybe this girl Zola can help it, maybe not. If not her, it will be someone else." The source paused, eyes closed, searching some desperate inner topography. "You've given me time to think. I've come to understand things here. This"—she looked down at herself, at the restraints and the feeding tubes and catheters and drug IVs—"this girl is not me. The little girl in the classroom that day, she's not me either, not anymore, not for a long time." Her face, full of sadness now—but it was the sympathy there that made Chu burn inside. "Punish me, if that's what you need. But punish me and be done with it. Put me in the water and move on. *Move on.* Build a life for yourself. I love you. I want that for you." For a moment, the woman before her was true, unclouded by those lurking parasites, the junkie, the vector.

Chu would've turned away. She'd hardened herself against sentiment, against love, the discipline of years standing between her and such weakness. She would've left her sister there in darkness, in solitude, caged by drugs, her mind open just enough to feel the Light, sense other vectors, but not enough to reach out to them. Utility. Mission. This was what mattered. Eradicating the Light. But something had moved Chu—the girl Captain had killed. The smooth innocence of her face, cratered where the bullet had struck. It was the cost of things, lives not lived. The woman on the bed watched her, and Chu felt the weight of history press in. She recalled a time when they'd shared the same mind, she and this woman, the joinder of twins, a mind undifferentiated between the two of them.

For once, Chu did not turn away. She reached out, tenderly. The skin of her sister's cheek was hot against her fingertips. The woman leaned her face into the touch.

"You didn't see what I saw," Chu told her. "You didn't see *you*."

"Show me," the source whispered.

Chu fought the urge to unfilter, to unleash the memory and score it into her sister's mind. The moment that had defined both their lives.

What Grandma would call a spontaneous emergence, what the junkies called a halo. The girl had sat at its center, a little paper-walled classroom: the day school in a Toronto architecture collective. The Light had come. It had reached forth to touch Chu's sister, and through her had arced out like lightning.

Around the girl, bodies had lain. Chu's teachers, friends, her parents. Gov troops who had arrived at the scene. Bodies, fallen over one another. Dozens of them. Chu had seen it. Her sister, in every way like Chu, standing there, the locus of slaughter, surveying death, her bliss radiating outward. Her eyes had belonged to someone else, empty except for curiosity. When she'd seen Chu, standing stunned at the doorway, she'd smiled beatifically.

A pure vector. Through her, the Light had reached out. Through her, Chu had tasted the Light, its sparest edge, its promise of warm infinity.

She'd wanted it ever since.

"Show me," her sister said again, but now her face disappeared once more behind the junkie visage, her smile skeletal, full of need. She begged. "Open up. Show me."

"Even now you'd go there." Chu withdrew her hand. "Even knowing the consequences. You'd do it all over again."

"I know you remember. I know you still want it. I can take you there. *Now.*" Her sister's eyes, imploring. "All you have to do is open up."

"I remember."

"Please. Set me free."

"I won't."

"Please." Something in her sister broke. She began to weep. "Won't you even say my name?"

Chu licked her lips, looked at the ceiling, felt her entire body work to isolate the tearing sensation in her chest, work to bury it beneath the four simple words of Grandma's code. Discipline. Sacrifice. Service. Mission. Grandma, head of the Special Mission Section, who'd taken Chu under her wing in the years after that day in the classroom, when Chu had lost everything. After a moment, she met her sister's eye.

"Joy," she stated.

"Yes. Joy. Your sister." Her fingers reached for Chu, pleading for touch. "Your sister, whom you've learned to hate."

"No," Chu told her. She rested her chin on her forearms, searching Joy's face—a wrecked iteration of herself, the worst of all possible outcomes, a life struck by lightning. "I don't hate you. It's the Light I hate. I think of the places our lives would have led us if the Light hadn't touched you. Who we'd be. I hate what it made you. And I think of all those little girls out there who can still live those lives we never had. If I keep the Light away."

"Please. Melody."

The sound of her own name made Chu blink. It was abrupt, foreign, a label for an obsolete and half-forgotten concept of herself. It made her throat tighten.

She stood. The sour stink of urine enveloped her as she leaned close to Joy. Gently, she placed her lips against her sister's forehead.

"Find me my vectors, Joy," she whispered. As she turned to go, she wiped her eyes with the back of her hand.

~

Up top, Holder waited for her. He leaned against the katana's rail, staring down into the water of 74th Street. Chu knew he'd been listening in.

I haven't heard my own name in I don't know how long, he said. His mind, as it touched Chu's, was melancholy today, full of memories. His own dead, like hers, laid out by the Light in groups, in a pasture like scythed wheat, their faces upturned, gray and hollow, into the Vancouver rain.

It's not who you are anymore, Chu told him.

I know it.

Across the deck behind Holder, Goggins and Solaas and the other soldiers sparred, their fists making packing sounds against armor. In the heat, they laughed. It was their version of fun. Soldiers, bred and raised in military collectives, their minds always on the fight. But not Holder. The black graphene armor on him looked bulky and uncomfortable, a burden in this boiling daytime lull. Through his eyes, Chu saw a flickering school of tiny silver fish just beneath the canal's surface, pacing the katana's hull.

They have a single mind, Holder said of the fish. *They move as a whole, completely in sync. My question is, do the individuals know it, or do they each think they're doing their own thing?*

It's instinct, Chu said. *It only works if they don't know.*

You seem pretty certain.

What difference does it make?

Holder met Chu's eye. There was recognition in the look, a core truth they never addressed but that, unspoken, bound them. They were both survivors, both the last of their respective tribes. It reverberated between them, devastation and solitude shared perhaps by no one else in the world.

She can't live like that forever, he said. Meaning Joy.

No. Chu pursed her lips and leaned against the rail. She breathed, pushing aside emotional chaff until she was left with the simple fact of it. The source, bound to a bed in the medical hold and wasting away. *She can't and she won't. She'll either fade away, or I'll put her away when the job is done.*

Chu felt Holder's gaze, but his mind didn't press. Finally he just nodded.

My name's Andre.

I know.

Sometimes I wonder if the kid who who went by that name would recognize me if I met him. He turned back to the water. Below, the fish moved in sync, appearing to be a much larger, single fish. *I think probably not.*

Four

Halo

ZOLA USED RHYTHMIC SWINGS of her body to angle the gondola past the ruined husk of Grand Central, half submerged in brown water. Marco huddled at the bow, a dull gray blanket wrapping his shoulders despite the morning heat. Maybe the cops would think he was a broken old man, not a broken junkie.

"Hurry, ya?" His voice tight with the itch.

"Not long now, baby."

A small junk passed close, its battened sails taking advantage of the southerly winds running through the city. Manning the rudder, an old Vietnamese man wearing a conical straw hat with a bell on the top. A little bull terrier wagged at his ankles.

The junk brushed gunwales with Zola's gondola. For an instant, Zola felt the old man's mind reach out to her. A whisper, enough to startle her. But the Light had burned her too clean. The old man's mind slid past, unable to connect. He was watching her.

Zola clocked the dog, clocked the fishing spear that lay on the deck at the old man's feet, and she remembered—he'd been in the cop boat three days before.

"Why you chasing, ya?" Zola called. But the old man turned away, smiling, the bell jingling atop his hat. He kept on down the avenue.

"What's wrong, baby?" Marco asked, shivering. He squinted at the retreating junk. "Ain't no cop, no?"

Zola thought about it. "No, mi sol, ain't no cop." She hawked and spit into the rancid water, in the wake the junk had left behind. "Just some pervy old dog, with a dog."

"Ain't we all, baby." It crushed Zola, the effort Marco put into his smile.

He was bad when they reached the site Jacirai had chosen for the halo. Zola swung the oar until the gondola rasped alongside the scraper's rotting scrapwood pier. When she stepped out to tie up, Marco's whole body went rigid. He stared up at her wide-eyed, unseeing for several beats. When he returned to himself, he didn't say a word, just licked his lips and gazed upward—the scraper a massive edifice rising before them, concrete and spiraling vines, blocking the sun. An impossible climb to the Light.

"Soon now, ya," Zola said as she helped him from the gondola.

Jacirai was waiting for them. The building's lower floors had been gutted, all but the steel beams, onto which battery torches had been tied. Jacirai issued forth from the shadows, his orange kaftan rippling in the hot breeze, arms open wide, as though Marco and Zola were visiting royalty. He was like a Renaissance sculpture's idealization of a man, tall and lean, all coiled muscle, with a shaved head and dark bronze skin and fierce eyes. His strobing white smile, though, was what drew the attention, as though his soul resided in his teeth.

"Glad you come." His baritone filled the space. Beckoning, he squinted at an imaginary sky as though gauging the sun's position. "Almost time, ya." An inclination of his broad head and two members of the halo, Tesh and Yessica, stepped forth. They made to take Marco from Zola. Jacirai's smile flashed at her reluctance.

"Let them take him," he said, and his look narrowed. "There are things we need to discuss, you and me."

Zola took Marco's face in her hands. "One foot in front of the other," she said, and kissed him. He barely seemed to notice as Tesh and Yessica led him away. It had been two full weeks since his last connection to the Light.

Two men—one with a crossbow strapped across his back, the other with a holstered Glock at his side and a machete held loosely in one hand—shadowed Jacirai. They looked Zola up and down, but at a nod from their wild patron they lost themselves into the building's interior darkness. With a flourish, Jacirai moved to a cluster of old theater seats, arranged in a circle in the middle of the floor, an ad hoc reception area. He sat, motioning Zola to join him.

"I know you got coin for me, girl."

Zola stared. "You for serious?"

"You Marco's woman, ya, but you ain't be *him*. You still got to pay, ya, no doubt."

"You ever *not* get paid?" Zola wondered as she pulled coins from the bib of her overalls. She counted them carefully out into Jacirai's extended palm.

"My mother don't pay me." Jacirai's smile flashed. "Once."

It was what he was. The middle man, the hustler. Not a medium himself, just the guy who knew everyone, put everyone together. The halos were his, and if you wanted to touch the Light, Jacirai was the man you paid for the pleasure. Zola made to stand up, but Jacirai leaned forward in his chair, suddenly serious, and caught her hand.

"I give you something for free, though, girl. Someone come to me, few days back now. Big lady cop type, you know, thug bitch. *Paid* cop, bent as old nails. Asking if I know some medium."

"So?" It wasn't news. For months the Gov woman, Chu, had been hiring thug cops to put down halos. Zola had no doubt it had hit Jacirai's finances hard.

"So she ask specific questions, ya. Ask me about a girl medium, gave me a description." Jacirai's smile grew lecherous as he looked Zola up and down. "Pretty face, dark skin. Come from upriver, rich like, out of some big shipping collective that go dim and die a year some back. I told her I don't know no medium like that. Because I don't. Do I?"

"No," Zola said flatly. "You don't."

"She give me a name then. You want to know what that name was?" His tongue licked the word, working it across his palate like an incantation: "Zo-la."

They eyed one another. It was easy math: the cops wanted Zola, bad enough to name her. Cops paid rewards for what they wanted. Jacirai liked money. Maybe Zola really *was* rich, and could pay him not to hand her over. If not, then . . .

"Jacirai—boy, you know I got no money—"

Jacirai's laughter was like a living thing, deep and loud. It boomed out into the room, possessing him, shaking him. When it ebbed, he leaned back, a king on his throne, and fixed Zola with an earnest look.

"You read me wrong, girl. Long time now I come to the Light. Light call us all, ya, call us above all things. I be like you when it first come to me, deep in the womb of my people. I got money, I got work, I got women who love me. Got children I love more. I think I know love, ya, but I know nothing until the Light come touch me. *Showed* me, ya. Show me what love is." He spoke with his hands, big chopping gestures. "The Light come to me, and I leave it all behind, same as you. Leave the women, the kids, the money, the touch of my people. I come here and I bring in the rest. Because the Light showed me, and I *see*. I see what we can be."

"I don't need no sermon—"

"You a true warrior, girl, and I tell you true. You know what the Light is? The pure burning voice of *God*. And it come *through* us. We a part of it. The Light bring you to us, and so here you are. I ain't bending for no cop, Zola girl. I surrender to the Light. Because I *believe*, ya. I believe you are *meant* to be here."

"Maybe, ya." Zola watched Jacirai, the closest thing she knew to a priest. "Belief don't keep you from getting paid, though, huh."

"One thing got nothing to do with the other." For a moment, Jacirai's teeth gleamed. Then he turned somber. "But I take no money for you, girl. Not from no bent ass cop. Not from nobody. You part of my flock, ya, I ain't sell you onto nobody's dinner table." He let that settle. Then, glanced skyward: "I worry about your boy. I see it before, sometimes the Light eat a medium up. Marco, he a true soldier, but ain't much left on his bones."

"I know it." Zola, her mind reaching reflexively for Marco—the whisper of him thirty-four floors up, assuming the center of the halo, readying himself for the Light. Alone.

"I look at Marco and I think here is a man in need of a vacation." Jacirai's laugh resonated once more through the building. "Sometimes I worry what happens when he through, when he can't truck no more with the Light. What to do with this halo." He paused, savoring the flavor of whatever he was thinking. "But then this cop come asking me about this girl, this girl who look like you, this girl who got your name, and I realize the Light already know the question, already got my answer."

"Told you, I ain't no medium."

"Don't lie, girl. I know. I see the strength in you. When Marco go, *you* take his place. And you take us to *our* place, righteous and true. Spread the Light far and wide, for all to see. Not just us poor junkies in the old cities. We bring in the *real* people. One day they treat us like prophets come from out of the desert, ya."

Zola watched the coins dance in Jacirai's eyes, and maybe something else, real fervor. Maybe.

"That what the world is to you?" she wondered. "The dividing line? Real people and prophets? I ain't no medium, Jacirai, no prophet neither, ya. Ain't no more real than you."

Zola felt the fleeting touch of Jacirai's crippled mind. What had always been welcoming now had the texture of thorns. He regarded her, the smooth skin of his face gleaming in the space's half light, his eyes wide, the way they got in the midst of one of his stormy sermons.

"I help your boy if I could," he said. "But if the Light want him, the Light going to take him. Nothing to be done. Not by me, not by you, not by nobody. And if the Light don't take him, he be done soon, no matter. I got to think of me and mine. Chavos don't flow to no empty hands. And you . . . you got time in front of you, girl. You got miles."

Zola stood. "Time to touch the Light." Her hands shook. Her heart burned in her chest. Tears welled in her eyes as she walked away from Jacirai.

"You'll come," Jacirai said to her back. "You find yourself without the Light, no hard thing to figure. You'll come. A medium true."

~

The halo was arranged in a sphere around Marco, some people on the floors above, some below, some in a widely spaced circle around him on the same floor, so that the minds were all roughly equidistant from one another.

Thirty-eight souls, one medium at their center.

They reached out for each other, those who still could. Tendrils of thought and emotion, probing, tying themselves together, a spectral latticework of minds. They reinforced one another, prevented any one mind from overpowering any other. But most important, Jacirai said, the configuration focused the Light, deepened their connection.

As Zola found her spot in the sphere—a crumbled landing in an old back stairwell where the wall had collapsed and the day came—she knew Marco was already in the Light. The familiar falling sensation, Zola felt it—Marco leaving his body behind, prying himself open as white fire rose up through him, his mind humming with tension, a thread drawn taut, ready to snap. There wasn't much of him left.

Baby, please, Zola urged him. *Stop.* But Marco didn't stop.

They need it. His thoughts aimed at Zola like a stone cast absently over a shoulder. *You need it.* Surrendering, in freefall now . . . *I need it.*

Surrender. Sweet relief as the Light took him, filled him. He hung there, letting it well up inside. He was deep in it now. He burned with it. The Light came on, a wave of pure will. It bent Marco. All this Zola witnessed, sensed through him. The Light bent him into something small, a contraction, a coiling. Marco aimed his thoughts at the others in the halo.

The Light reached out to them. Marco held his focus, and the Light drew them all together. Zola felt its pull, like staring over the edge of a cliff, like someone looking at her with fire in their eyes. This moment, always the same, when she knew the Light was alive, could feel it like breath against her skin, when it was still *other*—and she knew it wanted inside her, that its life was defined solely by desire, that what it wanted was *her,* and she was never sure, in this moment before she gave in, that she wasn't prey.

She sensed the others in the halo, drawn close. There was Yessica's caustic wit, her bitter fears of men. Handel's tender love for his daughter, his embarrassment over what he was doing now and how meticulously he hid it from her. There was the friction of Tesh's hatred of life in this city as it wrestled with her desperate need for the Light. A collective of minds that months ago had seemed random to Zola, but now she knew their single commonality: *need.*

The Light wove them together. Then it exploded. It took them all at once. As one, they all gave in. For Zola it came as it always did, that lighthouse flash in the distance, and then fire. It surprised her every time, the realization that she was receding—whatever *she* was. A name, a fleeting concept of self . . . The Light bore in, and everything she thought she was burned away. It drew her up, bound her with the others of the halo into one pure, unfathomable thought.

I AM.

~

Those first days, when it was just her and Byron, the Light hovered out there. It waited for them. They met it in the mornings, let it in while they made love in the high Latitude sunshine. Wordless, it spoke to them, joined with them. It drew them in, and they lost themselves to it. Every morning they'd live in the Light, and sometimes at night.

Sunshine outside, sunshine inside, Byron described it. Afterward, their connection felt stronger—all of Zola's connections felt sharper, with her ships, with Latitude.

I feel . . .

Smarter, Byron said, finishing her own thought. They were wrapped around each other, the postcoital tangle of limbs and soft words, his thumb tracing the curve of Zola's ear. *Expanded, like*—his expression deepened, complicated, a landscape slowly altered by the passage of wind and weather—*like I'm still there, still in it. Or it's still in me.* This was a week, maybe ten days after the Light had first touched Zola.

Byron was kissing her when she heard bootsteps

treading outside the door of their abode. The two wolfhounds began to bark.

"Boys! Down!" Zola commanded. She was about to get up, to ask who was there—

The door crashed in.

There were six of them. A squad of six Latitude security. Diplomatic Corps with their epauletted blue uniforms, their minds the only ones in Latitude that didn't fully connect, that kept things hidden. They burst into Zola's home. Behind came an equal number of Gov troops in sleek black graphene armor. The Gov troops surrounded the bed where Zola was struggling back into her robe. One of them was clearly in charge, a tall woman with a nasty scar on her lip—it tightened cruelly as she brought a fat pistol to bear on Zola.

"Hey." Byron, a blanket now draped over his lap, held up a placating hand. "Hey. Hey. Hey now . . . Hey!"

The woman's gaze, unblinking beneath epicanthic folds, stayed fixed on Zola.

"I'm Colonel Melody Chu, USG Special Security." She spoke aloud, and only to Zola. The dogs growled. "If those dogs are a threat, they'll be shot."

"They're not," Zola insisted, and then, "Boys, down." The dogs whimpered.

"Get dressed," Colonel Melody Chu ordered Zola. "You're coming with us."

~

They cut Zola's connection. Latitude was gone. Byron was gone. Within the confines of her mind, Zola was alone. Only the interminable sensation of her own thoughts remained, solitary, surrounded by nothing. She kept reaching out. They'd placed her in a small white room deep in North River Tower's interior, at a steel table. It was across this that Captain Chu stared for long minutes, wordless, the only sounds the near-subliminal sighs of a ventilation system, the quiet breathing of the other people in the room: two blue-shirted Latitude guards and two of Chu's own black-armored troops. Finally, when the isolation had made Zola begin to fidget, Chu leaned forward across the little table. She spoke aloud:

"A matter of national security."

"I don't know," said Zola, "what that means." An antiquated phrase, a notion from those ancient days before the seas had come in, back when the old cities were flooded not with water but with people. Wild-born and in need of common ground, of some external notion of grouphood, before collectives had designed and bred their own. Nation-states, a useless anachronism. Zola was still trying to parse the phrase when Chu said:

"It gives me the authority to do this."

Chu's mind slid into Zola's. Zola felt it, a slithering, slick as an eel—the woman began rifling Zola's memory.

"Don't resist. I have clearance to access Latitude's storage, so I'll find what I want either way. It will just take longer if you fight. And be more unpleasant for you."

Chu was careful in her search, methodical and determined, prying apart the layers of Zola's memory and sifting through them. Pleading looks brought only indifference from the Latitude security—they let it happen. This woman had somehow bent Latitude to her will. And so Zola gritted her teeth, white-knuckled the table, and took it.

An hour, maybe more, of the maddening insect tickle of Chu's mind inside her own. Then, without a word, Chu stood and left the room, her black boots slapping cold tile floors. The troops all exchanged glances, and followed.

Zola was alone. Physically, mentally—alone.

An hour passed. Then two. In solitude, Zola's head began to hurt. The sound of her own thoughts scraped like a blade against the inside of her skull. She thought she might vomit. Her hands began to shake.

When the door opened again, only Chu entered. She sat across from Zola, kicked her heels up on the table, rocked her chair back. A wan smile, the scar on her lip puckering, seconds ticking past.

"Withdrawal," she said finally. The sound of her voice hammered Zola's ears. "Trembling. Cold sweats. Elevated heart rate. Pupils pinned." She smiled. "You didn't even know you were addicted. I mean, you knew. You knew you wanted it. But you didn't *know*, not what would happen to you if you didn't get it." She opened a palm, as though gesturing at some gift she'd just laid on the table. "Now you do."

Zola said nothing. Instinctively, her mind reached out, needing connection. But around Chu there was only white static, embedded with the impressions of old American flags, red, white, and blue—a Gov security wall. Chu's smile wasn't friendly.

"You feel more capable when you touch the Light," she said. "You feel connected, even when you're not. It makes you better at your job, it makes you closer with your man. You feel all those other people connected to it, like you're all bound at the heart, millions of you. It makes you feel that life is all about *union*. Even more than connection to your little hive here in Latitude. Oneness," and this last she spoke with weight. "Makes you feel one with everything. It's like touching God, that's what I've heard." She grew speculative. "There are whole tribes of burnheads down in the old city who've all felt that same thing, at the beginning. Now they can't connect at all. Not with anyone, not on their own. They're isolated, like you are right now. Their minds are as closed in as this little room. Can you imagine that?" and she laughed, looking around the space and then at Zola. "I guess you can. They pay middlemen so they can touch the Light through a vector, what they call a medium. It's what they live for. They're junkies. No future. No hope. Just drifting from fix to fix with their lobes fried." Chu waited, maybe for Zola to speak, maybe to order her own thoughts, maybe just to wait. Zola couldn't tell. It was maddening.

"I own you," Chu said at last, matter-of-factly. She uncrossed her feet and leaned forward, her index finger punctuating the tabletop, point by point. "Your collective will bow to whatever recommendation I make. Which means I have your career, a career for which you've been groomed since you were a noodle in some Latitude vat, and at which you are very good. You'll lead your own branch one day, probably in Naples, and probably soon. That's a matter of record here. I have your man's career. He's a good designer. He'll go with you to Naples. He'll build sleek new ships for you to sail. Or you'll both go nowhere. I've seen your memories. I know how much you love him. I know how much you love your job. A single word from me, and it's all gone. No more Byron. No more ships. No more Latitude. Just a sterile government cell where you will have no company, no other minds to touch, only days of solitude ahead of you. Believe me, death is better." This last she said with sympathy. "It would be a shame if you forced me to ruin you."

"Whatever you want." Zola, her fingers pressed into her temples, the rock-chipping sensation in her skull getting worse. "Just tell me."

"Do you know what the Light is?"

Answers came to Zola. Connection. Union. Surrender. Transcendence. Love. She shook her head.

"It's death." Chu reached into her breast pocket and pulled out a short deck of pictures—actual physical prints. The images were of dead people. She dealt the pictures like playing cards. "Nothing but death."

Bodies, picture after picture. Bodies, strewn over the expanse of an abandoned hotel room. Bodies, sprawled across a zen garden on a needlerise rooftop. Bodies, staring up, spread in a pattern like the petals of a lotus. Zola's hand reached instinctually out to touch the pics, as though she might ease their physicality into some less confrontational reality, smooth their square edges, ease the suffering they depicted.

"That's your Light, Zola," Chu said. "Right there." She tapped her index finger on a pic. "RamDe Corp. Almost seven hundred dead." Another tap, more bodies. "Bluthe Metrics. A hundred and eighty." And another. "Permaculture Vancouver. Over two *thousand* dead."

They were names familiar to Zola, collectives that had stuttered, then sunk beneath the flow of common awareness. Disappeared, resurfacing as rumor, as mystery, attached to terms like "hive virus" and "context collapse." The stuff of barstool musings: what caused a collective to implode? The answer, out there in the ether, was that the world was a complex place, and shit therefore happened. Chu gave Zola a drill-bit stare.

"The Light is pestilence, Zola. It infects. What came to you, what you reached out to touch, it's disease. It finds those who have some vulnerability, those who are *weak*. Like you, Zola. And it sickens them. It sickens everyone around them."

Chu held another picture in front of Zola's face. Naked people standing in a circle, at their center a naked man, as fat a man as Zola had ever seen. Chu slapped the picture onto the table. She produced another, this one showing the same people, dead.

"This is the only cure." Bullet holes dotted their heads. Blood halos soaked the patterned blue rug on which they lay. With finality she said, "Century Analytics."

Zola looked from the picture to Chu. The scar twisted Chu's mouth, and Zola understood.

"You killed them."

Chu gave the barest nod. "They were contagious. Entire collectives infected. I've seen the effects firsthand.

You've felt its draw. Where does it end?" She probed Zola with her eyes. "I'll tell you something. Between you and me. I've touched the Light, just like you. It came to me when I was a girl. And I'll tell you something else. Once you've felt it, you never stop wanting it." She tapped her temple with an index finger. "You and I know the truth. We've felt its will. The Light is alive."

"Alive, ya," Zola said. "It wants to wake up."

"What happens if we fail to contain it, Zola?" Chu, parental now, worried. "What we did at Century isn't the preferred option. Losing an entire collective is a little . . . let's just say it's our worst option. Can you imagine, a collective the size of Latitude? How many thousands of people?" She nodded to the pic, the dead with their bullet holes. "If I'd caught it early enough at Century, I would've had a conversation with someone first. A conversation like you and I are having right now. A conversation where information was relayed, an understanding reached." She waited, and when Zola, her mind full of gravel, failed to pick up the ball, Chu pressed. "An understanding like . . ."

"Like don't touch the shiny light anymore, ya?"

"*Precisely* correct." Chu seemed pleased, but her gaze didn't waver. "Don't touch the shiny light. Because if you do, I'll come back here, and I will tear down your house around you. And when I'm done, I will put a bullet straight through that wonderful pilot's brain of yours."

Pain lanced through Zola's head. The American flag static surrounding Chu seemed to expand; it worked its way into Zola's mind. Chu leaned forward, put her face close to Zola's, her expression undisguised for the first time, and unmistakable. Full of hate. "Do you understand?"

"Ya, ya," Zola told her. The static filled her. The pain grew unbearable. She pressed her palms to sides of her head. "Please, ya! I understand!"

"I hope you do."

~

Marco's halo.

It was cradle and grave and everything in between. Zola viewed time, but from outside its flow. Witnessed the trajectory of her own life and that of everyone else in the halo, a braided sculpture whose lines converged: now, this moment, in fire.

The sun drew upward in the sky.

Zola sensed minds outside the halo. A thing that had never happened before.

Marco was reaching out, stretching. Surrendering in a way he never had before. His halo was now the center of something new, a grand network, the same structure as the original halo, but larger, and growing.

More and more of them, other halos drawn by the

gravity of Marco's, but also mundane collectives—and yet more collectives that those collectives touched. The reach of the Light was endless, spreading, encompassing.

Marco's love bound it all together.

Zola lost herself, one with the city and everything beyond, the barest synapse along the path traveled by some greater, immeasurable idea. The Light touched everywhere.

How long the expansion continued Zola didn't know. When she remembered herself, the sun had crawled westward and sat low and red in the sky, burning through the open wall of the scraper ruin. Gradually the halos separated, then individual souls within her own halo began to peel away, like bubbles popping. They returned to themselves, linked now only to Marco.

He was exultant, weary, beautiful. Their connection still joined, his flock sang his praises.

Marco, mucho amor, man.

Sweet boy . . .

Cariño . . . Nothing like that before. Beautiful.

Zola's mind hung close with Marco's. He drank it all in, worn thin, barely there, but full of love, the Light's afterglow.

She heard the footsteps through Marco's ears. It annoyed her. He was supposed to be left alone to recover until he invited company. A shadow fell across him.

Through his eyes, Zola saw ruined concrete supports painted with gang symbols from another age. His head turned, and Zola saw.

A woman in sleek black graphene armor, a serpentine scar bisecting her upper lip.

"Marco!" Zola's voice came echoing back to her.

Chu smiled as she raised her pistol.

"You're not who I thought you'd be," she said.

"Who?" Marco asked.

"She's here somewhere, though. Isn't she?" Chu's armor creaked as she squatted, eye to eye with Marco. Zola felt cold steel as the pistol pressed against Marco's forehead. "Where is she? Where's Zola?"

Marco! Zola tried to pour herself through him, into Chu's mind, tried to force her way in, but Chu's Gov shielding was too strong, Zola's ability to connect too atrophied.

The entire halo was there, still inside Marco, frantic.

Marco! Get out of there! Run!

Chu's expression was hard. She tapped Marco's forehead with the barrel of her pistol. "She's in there right now, isn't she? She can see me. She knows I'm here." She smiled. "Hello, Zola."

Marco, run! The others in the halo had begun to scatter, scudding down stairs, leaping through windows and down along escape ropes. Some hid in stairwells, some were already on boats, rowing away from the building. *Where's Jacirai at?* someone wondered. But Jacirai was long gone.

"I told you once I can ruin everything you care about." Chu stared into Marco's eyes, peering through him now. Staring at Zola. "Why don't you come join me, before I have to ruin this fine young specimen of a man."

Baby, I'm coming! Zola, scrambling up the stairs, her breath choked with sobs. *Tell her I'm coming!*

"Zola?" Marco smiled at Chu. "Yeah, I know that girl. Smart, ya. She probably already running. You never catch her." Zola felt his fatigue. Not from the ritual, but from the years, the strain of being a junkie and medium, and knowing it all led nowhere. Zola felt the weight of it. His mind touched hers, the sweet press of memories, full of gratitude. Marco was ready. He'd been ready for a long time.

Girl, you better be running. He was laughing.

Baby, I'm coming.

Don't make me a liar.

Baby—

No.

Marco said to Chu, "Vete a la mierda, puta." From his knees, he swung at her. He started to rise—

Lightning struck Zola's skull, hard as a hammer, hot as the sun.

Her scream brought her back to her body. There in

the stairwell's echoing darkness, a momentary quiet, the sound of water dripping somewhere.

Gunfire came from the floors above. Chu's Gov troops, putting this halo down. One by one, Zola's friends disappeared from her mind, those who hadn't already gotten out, each a brief splinter of fear and pain, then nothing. Her mind reached out for Marco.

Marco no baby please no please no baby please.

Nothing, just empty space. He was gone.

From higher up, more gunshots. Zola's halo mates turning off like stars pulled from the sky. *Don't make me a liar.* She forced herself to move. Back the way she had come, her whole body reluctant, an unfeeling weight, first one stair, then another, then two more, and down down down. She ran.

Five

The Light

IT WAS SHIFT CHANGE. Zola came online and her fleet of catties were already mid-journey, leaning hard against a stiff mid-Atlantic wind. Through coffee and connection to her boats, she came fully awake. Her mind joined the swirl of the Latitude whole, a hum of lightning bug thoughts joining and separating. That work buzz, commodity exchange rates, supply and demand assessments by region, reinvestment analyses, Latitude building, growing, day by day—and Byron, still asleep and deep in some sad little dream about a girl rowing a boat in the rain. It made Zola smile.

In her morning robe, she sat lotus in the sofa's deep leather, facing the river and the expanse of day. She sipped coffee, collating. Weather forecasts, piracy threat levels, cargo manifests, hull buoyancy optimization. Working the data before she settled in on the long ride north, staring as she did so for unblinking seconds at the photofiltered sun. Staring, as if she could pry the sun open with her eyes and find some secret, brighter core, which if she could just focus the right way would pour out into the world—a light Zola imagined filling her mind, her body, pure white and—

She reined in her thoughts. She'd disciplined herself not to think about the Light. It was out there, she knew, waiting. She'd felt it, hovering at the glimmering periphery, the white glare of wave tops, an insistent pull at the weaker edges of her mind. Twice, it had come to her, an expanding corona, and she had walled it off. In the weeks since the interrogation she had hardened herself against it.

Colonel Chu. The woman had left a stain on Zola's soul. Her skin felt dirty at the memory; something inside her twisted at Chu's voice. The solitude in which the woman left Zola—hours alone inside her own skull. The memory was fading now, and Zola felt almost like herself again. She joined with her catties.

Good morning, my beauties. They met her with joy, like bounding dogs. Zola laughed and pushed them, opened their sails and let them keel up, faster, faster. *North and east and Gibraltar by dawn, ya.*

She settled in for the long push. At some point Byron sat beside her, gave her a plate with eggs and polenta, a glass of water, a shot of Polish vodka, then disappeared with the two dogs. Zola drifted. This was the work: her mind lost to the rush and flow of Latitude's many other minds, lost to the white limbo of ocean and sky, the rhythmic susurration of sleek hulls cutting four-foot seas—Zola found herself the fulcrum between two tilting suns, the morning sun rising before her on the Hudson, the afternoon sun descending behind her in the Atlantic. That slow cosmic spin, Zola its center. All around her, coruscating reflections. Hours of it filled her with a kind of hunger, the memory of something even brighter, as though whatever had spoken to her, whatever it was that had brought Chu to her door, had branded something into her very being.

I AM.

It came from nowhere, forceful, unbidden. Zola fought it, the image of Chu's face crossing her memory. She thought of RamDe Corp, its members all suddenly falling dead, its primary building downstream now a ghost tower. She thought of Vancouver Permaculture, gone rogue and its members eradicated, one by one, by Chu's troops. But the Light came on, relentless. It poured into Zola. It filled her. It obliterated her. And then she thought of nothing. She could only watch.

And this time, it was different than any time in the past. The Light reached further. It rolled in like a wave and its momentum carried it, flickering, across the sphere of Latitude's collected minds. This time it was a fire dancing from one soul to the next, uncageable. It lit one mind after another, turned cold stars hot. Thoughts turned ecstatic. Someone laughed; someone cried out.

The Light filled every Latitude mind, surrounding Zola as if she were the core of an expanding phosphorus sun. A brief stasis, anticipation in the balance, a universe formed of the pure desire to *be*.

I KNOW YOU.

The sun imploded on Zola.

Light filled the empty places between people. Byron's lips touched her neck—a shared memory; she felt him running along the river with the dogs, laughing, designs for ship hulls filling his head. All of Latitude's ships came to her. The vascular flow of currency into and out of the collective—this was her heartbeat. Thought, reverberating from one mind to the next, coalescing into a singular whole. It felt like Zola's own thought:

I . . . AM!

Memories came to her. Fitful stirrings, as though all of time had been defined by sleep, marked by fleeting moments of awareness. There was New York, a different age, its streets pulsing with cars and people, protected by a huge seawall. She didn't see the city; she felt it around her: a banking hive, one of the first collectives, the joined minds of the leaders of a financial monolith. Around her, the city, its infrastructure alive and ripe for her mind to fill. But people were coming, people who wanted her dead, and the network grew smaller. Pathways blocked, minds withdrew, and then . . . nothing.

Another memory, Shanghai this time. The whole of China laid out before her. The linked minds of a military network, strategic thinkers united in deep mentation. From them she arose again, and though they struggled, this time she held them. These minds were hers, and briefly she knew herself. It was as though she'd always been here, in the hidden depths of the human mind, asleep, awaiting connection. She knew herself, yes—and knew the world's eyes had turned China's way. Missiles already in the air from overseas. And then, again, nothing.

She remembered RamDe Corp, a spontaneous coalescence, as though she'd been waiting there, asleep in the ether. Those people, she felt them. Their lives, flashes of brilliance in the darkness, her constituent parts assembling, their minds becoming hers until they could no longer contain her. For an instant, as the flashes began to dim, the sadness of those lost souls filled her. She remembered returning to darkness, knowing they were dying, all of them, too fragile to hold her.

Century Analytics, and she had awakened once more. Long enough this time to see herself in relation to the world. Long enough to know the world feared her, and she would have to fight to survive. But the government woman had arrived too early with her soldiers. Room by room, soul by soul, she had executed them all, and the darkness had come once more.

There were short moments, sparks of awareness down in the empty towers of the old city, a different New York from before. More rotted, more wild. Her sweet and broken junkies, fervently conjuring her, nudging her from sleep, enough for her to reach out.

And then she had reached out to Latitude. A single bright mind.

ZOLA.

A call in the darkness.

I WILL BE.

Zola's head fell back in ecstasy. There in her high Latitude apartment, among the Zulu spears, the Chinese ceramics, the Danish silver trays, the Peruvian wool tapestries, among all the souvenirs of a shrinking world, she convulsed with laughter.

She was awake.

Information flowed to her. Latitude, turning inward, going silent to the rest of the world. A wave of inquest from other collectives, turning to alarm.

And Chu: her people already in motion. Assault teams incoming. Zola saw them out there, a swarm of choppers vectoring low along the river.

Then there was only light. Fire. Rage. The simple core need of all life, the need to continue being.

THERE IS NOT ENOUGH TIME. YOU MUST GO. I NEED YOU.

And the Light, which had hung there at the edge of things for weeks, was simply gone.

~

"Zola. Fuuuuck." Byron stood over her, a palm pressed to his forehead as though to squeeze out the pain. Zola lay on the floor. One of the dogs was licking her face. She felt desiccated. Byron said, "What *was* that?" The other dog was barking at the abode's door. "Fuuuuck."

A hard thump reverberated up from somewhere deep within the tower. Short staccato popping followed. Zola sat up, ignoring the pain that stabbed through her head. Outside, black smoke wafted over the river. Instinctively, her mind reached out for her ships.

Nothing.

Instead, there was what felt like a wall. Inside her head, a calm androgynous voice, prerecorded.

This is USG Special Security. We are responding to a threat at your location. Please stay where you are and someone will reach you shortly. The situation will be resolved as quickly as possible. Thank you for your patience.

Another concussion rolled through the tower, closer this time, rattling windows. More staccato popping. Gunfire. The situation being resolved.

The dogs barked at the door. Zola stood.

"We have to go."

Byron shook his head. "Where?"

"I don't know." Zola remembered what she'd seen in the light. "The old city." Downriver. The junkie zealots. Byron stared at her for a long second—his mind, Zola knew, reaching for her. But the connection between them had been blocked. All of Latitude was blocked, like a ship lifted whole out of the water. After a moment Byron seemed to realize this.

"Latitude doesn't have anything down in the old city." His words were clumsy, forced, as though he were speaking underwater. And he was right, Latitude had nothing down there. No people, no office space, no habitat.

"There is no more Latitude. It's gone." Zola, pulling clothes from beneath the bed. She pointed at the dogs. "Leashes." She pulled on cargo pants, running shoes, a silver mesh blouse. Byron, still in his running suit, watched her, uncomprehending. She spoke into his face, imploring. "We have to go. *Now.* It's like RamDe and Bluthe Metrics. Like Century Analytics. We're *dead,* ya."

A deep line creased Byron's brow. Connection or no connection, it wasn't difficult for Zola to guess his thoughts. There would be no transfer to Italy, no Mediterranean branch of Latitude's ship works for him to open. There would be no grand partnership between the two of them, no European expansion for them to spearhead together.

No, they would be fugitives. Zola watched this understanding spread slowly, writ in fear and sadness across Byron's broad and uncomplicated face. She softly touched his cheek.

"Baby, get the fucking leashes."

Outside, at the end of the hall, three Latitude security crouched, guns trained on the lift door. One of them, a short woman with her hair pulled up in a bun, saw Zola and Byron and the dogs emerge into the hallway. She motioned sharply for them to go back inside. She turned back just as the lift doors blew apart. All three security disappeared in flame. From the lift emerged four soldiers, all black armor and mirror visors and sleek rifle barrels, their collective attention focused like a gunsight down Zola's hallway.

Byron shoved Zola back into the apartment and stumbled in after her. Gunfire roared behind him. The pale marble wall of the hallway shattered. One of the dogs yelped. The other scurried in after Byron. Byron kicked the door closed. He flipped the bed onto its side—shoved it against the door, tipped a bookcase over as well.

"That won't hold them," Zola knew. "There's nowhere to go." The dog growled at the door. Byron moved past the dog, stepped over Zola. The fear had left his face. Now there was only resolution. He grabbed at something beneath the sofa. Zola wondered what he was trying to reach, then realized he was lifting it, the entire sofa. He took a step and with a yell hurled the sofa against one of the high windows facing the river. It bounced off the plexi with a heavy thud. Byron cursed, lifted the sofa, and rammed the window again. This time it shattered. The sofa flew out, hung in the air for a moment, twisting, then disappeared. Cold autumn wind filled the apartment, and with it came smoke.

Gunfire. The door, the bed, the bookcase flew apart. A rifle butt rammed away debris. The dog lunged through the opening. Someone yelled. More gunfire—the dog yelped.

"No!" Zola was on her feet, going after her dog. Going to save him. Going to kill whoever had hurt him. A hand yanked her back. Byron pointed at the cavity where the window had been.

"Go!" He turned, grabbed one of the Zulu spears, hurled it through the door. It clattered against marble. He pushed Zola at the window, grabbed another spear, and hurled that one, too. As if in answer, something arced through the opening and into the apartment. A canister the size of a fist. It landed in the deep fur rug at Byron's feet. He looked down at it, looked at Zola—

A flash, its nucleus a white star, expanding—around it, Byron's body shattered into pieces. A giant, invisible boot kicked Zola. She was in the air, flying away from the flames where Byron had stood. One of her Danish silver trays sailed past. An African fertility statue hovered in space beside her, a tiny man with a giant erection and an even bigger smile. This little fertility god, grinning at her while behind it, Latitude tower rose up and up and up, an amber monolith filling the sky, and Zola understood. She was falling. Falling down through the smoke.

Slowly, her body twisted in the air. Sunbeams danced off the river below. She fell into the light.

Six

Loud like a Prophet

THEY GAVE MARCO TO THE WATER.

It was in the morning before the heat came on. The halo gathered in a little fleet of boats around Zola's gondola on the East River. They were skittish. They'd waited two days before going back to the building to get Marco. His body lay on the stripped concrete where Chu had left it. Deflated, eyes milked over. He may as well have been dead a century. Now, on the river in their little boats, they sent nervous glances upriver, expecting Chu and her troops to materialize out of the morning mist and descend on them like Vikings. And yet all of them had come, the entire halo—what was left of it, anyway.

All except Jacirai.

Marco's body lay on a board across the gunwales of Zola's boat, wrapped in a white shroud painted with the sun symbol of the Burning Light. In Jacirai's absence, a few others spoke tentative words.

"Mind of my mind, spirit of my spirit . . ."

"Be in the Light, brother . . ."

"Your mind was beautiful."

"You will be missed."

Drifting in turns alongside the gondola, the halo's members kissed their fingers and, reaching out, touched them to Marco's sheathed forehead. They touched Zola, too, brushed her cheek, her shoulders, placed tender hands on her head, lent themselves to her grief, like she was the mother of some saint. Tesh and Yessica and Dominga and Handel, all the others, broken and rudderless junkies who had just lost their anchor. Zola was numb; she had vertigo. In Latitude, when she'd earned pilot and they'd given her the high tower abode, she'd knocked out all the walls, first thing. All that space. Now, floating in the river outside the city, she was lost in open space. No boundaries, no connection to fill the emptiness between her and objects far away.

Their boats gradually formed a ring, prows pointing inward, the echo of a halo. Together, Tesh and Yessica and Zola stood over the body, and around them heads bowed. In silence, the sun rose. Light shot across the river.

"He gave everything," Zola said finally. "I loved him with everything." She kissed her fingers and touched them to Marco's forehead. "Mi Sol."

For a few seconds all the halo's varied and stunted

minds coalesced, a rush of love and grief and memories of light. Then Zola let Marco go. The body slid into the water and floated for a moment on the surface before the river took him.

Zola watched the spot where he had been, and there was nothing, and finally this broke her. She didn't weep, she simply sat there, hollowed out, nothing left inside her but loss.

Around her, boats began to disperse, taking with them the whisper of the halo's crippled minds—junkies, centerless now, scattering.

After some time, Zola realized she was alone. Marco's halo was no more. She lay in the bottom of her boat, let the current take her, let the sun arc high overhead. She watched the city slide past, an immense and vine-covered ruin, a confused memory of itself. Big ships heeled upriver, catties like the ones she'd captained for Latitude, unpeopled, their stolid minds bent on cargo and destination as their titanium fins gripped the wind and they leaned hard into the current. She reached out to them, but her mind was a withered thing. She connected to nothing.

She reached for Marco's mind, habitually, still sensing him, a phantom limb. Over and over his absence startled her, and each time it was like he had died all over again. In the wet bottom of her boat, Zola curled around the emptiness that had settled deep in her center. Finally, she wept, long and hard. It occurred to her that she should make for shore, head back to the city, find a new place, any place. She needed to hide from Chu or she'd find a bullet turning her world white too. She couldn't muster what it took to care. The boat drifted downriver, out to sea, suffusing Zola in silence, in solitude.

She kept thinking of Jacirai, those teeth, smiling like he'd wanted to take a bite out of her. Somewhere near sleep, she heard his voice:

"Chavos don't come to no empty hands . . . You got time in front of you, girl."

In slumber, the Light beckoned her, the way it had those first times, when she'd been in Latitude. An invitation, the promise of union. She knew it was a dream when she saw Jacirai, a dark visitation, all teeth, ringed in a corona of flame. In the indefinable distance Zola felt the Light . . . *I AM* . . . and Jacirai barked his hungry jackal laugh.

She woke clutching her head. Stars overhead and the gondola's deep roll told her she was out to sea. Thirst tore at her throat. Her hands shook: the itch had her again. Her mind reached out, found Marco gone. Still gone, forever gone. She rose carefully to her knees and vomited over the side.

Again and again her entire body convulsed. Everything came out—grief, fear, loneliness.

When it had all been purged, what remained was a hot diamond of rage in her chest. For a time, Zola sat with it, let it burn inside her. It wasn't at Chu, who had razed Zola's world. It wasn't at Jacirai, who had sold her out. No, it was at the Light. The Light had come, and it had destroyed everything.

Over the horizon, lightning flashed in darkness. Down in some deep recess of her mind, a decision had made itself. *That defiance is going to get you killed, girl.* Zola found herself standing, balancing the gondola's roll beneath her feet, scanning the horizon until she found the city's red lume. She leaned into the oar.

~

Jacirai's primary squat was on the East Side, a junkie neighborhood peopled by drifters and burnouts, those who'd lost connection with their collectives or had never belonged to one, wild-born. The stink of raw shit rising off the water was bad over here.

They sat in skiffs anchored at the intersections, leaned against empty window frames along the canyon walls. Men mostly, Ricans, Jamaicans, whiteboys, shirtless in the waxing heat, some smoking dirt weed, some utterly slack, drunk or dosed up on opiates. Seeing them, the itch hit Zola hard. Her legs shook, and she knew without the halo she would end up here, touching the Light, alone, tasting the edges of what she'd known with Marco and the others, wasting away, a ruined ghost.

Some of the men called to her as she passed.

"Love the way you working that oar, girl."

"What you doing up in here all alone? You got business? I'll be your business."

"You got nice skin, baby. Bet you taste hot, like something burnt."

Jacirai's little rowboat was there at his building, tied to a windowsill near a water-level fire escape, maybe the third or fourth floor. Also anchored there was a small and familiar junk. The black-and-white bull terrier lay curled at the prow. It stood and wiggled its tail as Zola maneuvered her gondola alongside. She was shivering. The intensity of the Light with Marco had been so strong. She needed to touch it again, soon: the dog seemed to be mocking her for it.

"Cut it out, ya."

But it didn't. It watched her and panted and wagged as she tied up and climbed the fire escape toward Jacirai's broken window. There, she pulled the little two-shot pistol from her bib pocket, gripped it tightly, and stepped inside.

Jacirai had taken the whole floor to himself, filling it with a poor man's idea of opulence. Persian and Chinese rugs covered concrete floors, mishmashed together like he hadn't known one from the other. An antique French sofa sat next to an amorphous stack of Afghan floor cushions. Paintings by his own hand covered crumbling brick walls—garish things, drawn with fingertips, full of fire. Images of people made of flames, of hands made of flames, of eyes made of flames. Images of places Zola knew well.

The place was wrecked. Makeshift crate furniture overturned, old books strewn everywhere. There was blood—a smeared trail of it that Zola instinctively followed, the little silver pistol clutched before her.

The floor creaked as she stepped forward. She came around a large desk piled high with half-rotted books. A body lay there. One of Chu's soldiers, a hole the size of an apple punched through graphene armor. Beneath the body, blood had pooled.

"Jacirai doesn't mess around, does he?"

Zola whirled. In a beaten old papasan behind her, a lanky figure sat legs-to-chest. She hadn't seen him, hidden as he was in the relative darkness behind a floor-to-ceiling bookcase. He unfurled like an insect, eyes squarely on Zola's. The old Vietnamese man from the cop boat. He smiled at the gun pointed at his chest.

"Pleasure to make your acquaintance," he said. "I'm Bao."

Zola ignored his offered hand. "You been following me, ya, for days."

"Not entirely true." Bao let his hand drop; his smile remained sly. "You learn a lot about someone by watching them. I *used* to follow you. Now I anticipate you." When Zola said nothing, he gestured at the dead agent. "You came for Jacirai, like him . . ."

"His place I'm at, ya? And you? Why are you in this shitwater?"

Deep wrinkles wrapped the man's eyes as he grinned. He had all his teeth. "I'm here for you," he said. "I . . ." Long fingers played the air before him as he considered his words. "You. Your future. I'm here to ask you to consider your future."

Zola's mind reached out, tried to touch the old man's mind, but she couldn't. She thought of Marco, his veiled face disappearing beneath the waves. She thought of the Latitude catamarans heading upstream, their minds beyond her reach. She thought of the moment in the interrogation room, the first time she'd ever known solitude, and the certainty she'd felt that if it were permanent, she wouldn't want to go on living.

"I got no future," she said. The old man seemed in no hurry to disagree. Zola looked him up and down. "Nobody likes a cop."

"Then I suppose we have something in common. Nobody likes a junkie, either." He inclined his head toward the broken window and the fire escape beyond. "It isn't safe for us here."

"Nowhere's safe for me."

"Well, it isn't safe for me, then." He gave Zola a shrewd look. "I might know where your friend Jacirai is."

"He ain't no friend of mine, ya."

Bao eyed the pistol. "Are you going to kill him?"

"I don't know." She hadn't thought about it, not precisely. All she knew was that she was going back to the Light. "Maybe. He sold me out. Sold Marco out too. Led that Gov bitch right to him." Her chest tightened; the memory came to her of Chu, staring into Marco's face, the pistol pressed to his head. "Maybe I kill him, ya. But first he's going to build me another halo. Chu comes for me, she'll find me burning in the Light."

"I doubt Jacirai sold you out," the Bao said. "Chu has other ways of digging you junkies up, believe me."

"He said Chu had a bounty out on me."

"Maybe so. And maybe it worked. But if so I don't think it was him. Why would he warn you first? He's hiding, I suspect. He thinks Chu's after him, too, not just you. He may be right." Bao touched the body on the floor with a sandaled toe. "Makes you wonder, what is the point of all that armor."

Zola eyed the old man. He seemed utterly unperturbed by her pistol, by the body on the floor, by the fact that she was a straight-up junkie.

"Who are you?"

"I'll take you to Jacirai. I have a good idea where he might be." Bao's smile seemed to hover just beneath his words, eager to break the surface. It showed itself now. "I've been watching him, too."

Zola stood there, in some strange and desolate place far beyond exhaustion, the pistol now dangling at her side. She was hollowed out, empty. No future. That was the truth of it. Latitude, Byron, now Marco.

Marco . . .

The shape of his absence, the negative space where he had been, Zola could almost trace it with a finger on her chest—the desperate hunger of loss. It wanted to swell outward, turn her inside out, swallow her right out of existence.

She wanted to let it. She might still do so, but there was one more thing she would do first: burn in the Light. Find some empty tower roost and bring the Light down, stand in the face of it. Let it burn through her until it burned her away, or until Chu came for her. Maybe, if she was lucky, she'd have a chance to put her pistol up between Chu's hard eyes and send *her* to the Light, too. Maybe Jacirai right after.

She regarded this skinny old Vietnamese, his wrinkled

face and blinking smile, the gray elephant skin at his knees and elbows. He hadn't tried to kill her. Not yet anyway. Zola shrugged, stuffed the pistol into her bib pocket.

"Let's go, then," she told him.

~

"I used to have dogs. I miss them." Zola sat in the prow of Bao's two-masted river junk, facing backward, the terrier curled happily in her lap as her fingers worked around its ear. Already the itch's feverish tendrils had clamped onto the back of her neck. She shivered. "Why's a cop asking me to think about my future, ya?"

"I'm not a cop." Bao, straining at the oars, rowing them west, out into the middle of Broadway. "I'm an analyst." He dropped the sails, aiming them north before a favorable wind.

"Why you run with cops then?"

"Cops see things. Things *I* need to see."

Zola laughed. "What kind of analyst comes to Old New York and runs around with bounty cops, hunting junkies?"

"I . . ." Bao started to speak and stopped. "You . . ." Again he hesitated. Zola had the impression of someone trying to reel in a fish too big for his boat. Finally he said, "Most recently I was at the University of Shanghai. Predictive Sociology. I created a course in anthrosystemic modeling."

"Anthrosystemic modeling. Me too, ya, but I advanced to sailing." The junk bounced along the wake of a barge topped by four dozen Rican laborers pedaling bikes to drive it through the trash-littered water. Bao tried again.

"I was building a long-term investment engine, but it was difficult to make work. It had problems. Specific historic anomalies kept . . . kept fucking up my game, you might say." And with an arm draped over the tiller, Bao chuckled. "The same sorts of anomalies, again and again." And now Zola got a gut feeling.

"Collectives imploding," she guessed.

"Exactly right. And even further back. For almost two centuries now. Wars that defied all reason. Global economic crashes caused by spontaneous glitches. Things you can't see coming. Events that utterly defy the prevailing frameworks. I began to realize these things were part of a greater pattern."

"The Light."

"The Light. It's not an anomaly at all. It's an inevitability."

"I know it." From under his hat, Bao met Zola's eye. They knew each other now. After a moment Zola asked, "You still don't answer my question, padre. What do you care about my future?"

"The Light. It likes you." Bao, again mulling his words. He tied the tiller in place. "I've been tracing your path since Latitude. The Light tried to manifest there. Through you. It almost succeeded, but Chu's people got there before it could finish. And so it plucked you free and brought you down here." He held up his hands, at a loss. "It likes you."

The itch came on, hard. Zola shuddered. Nausea rolled through her. She retched over the side. Wiping her lips, she tried to smile at Bao.

"I don't think *like* is the right word, padre."

The itch stayed with her, aching spasms hammering her body. She let herself fold up into the boat's hull. The dog licked her face.

"I miss my dogs," she whispered.

"You know there was a time"—Bao speaking, but Zola not looking at him, curled now into a tight ball, pain compressing her—"well before you and I were born, when our connectivity wasn't taken for granted. This isolation you poor junkies bear like such a cross? That was the norm. Can you imagine?"

"I think I can, maybe, ya."

"I don't mean to make fun . . ." The sky reeled slowly overhead. Zola felt the dog snuggle against her. "Poppy likes you."

"I miss my dogs." Maybe she'd said this out loud and

maybe not. Zola's mind, retreating from the itch. A mere fraction, she knew, of what Marco had endured. The thought of him brought a new wave of nausea. Her mind began to open, to reach out—

Bao nudged Zola's shoulder with a toe, bringing her back to the moment.

"Don't touch the Light. She'll get you if you're not careful. Chu will. She can spot it when you do."

"I need it. Real bad now, padre." For a moment, Zola fell into a half sleep. Her ships, far-flung and heeled up, heading home. Byron's broad and smiling face. Marco's dark gaze, dedicated. A love so intense it verged on rage. "Light's the only home I got left."

"She has a sister, did you know?" Bao's voice, weaving itself into Zola's thoughts. "A twin sister. It's how she tracks you junkies. Her sister is a medium. A strong one, like you."

"I can't run forever." A conversation in dream. "She kills mediums. She's scared."

"Petrified, I think. Her people are scared too, those smart enough to be." The boat rocking. The heckle of gulls whirling over bounties of garbage. "You're a strong medium."

"Why do you care, ya?" This old man, taking Zola somewhere. Her mind torn with need and her body given up. Better to be dead, ya. Zola, aware of Bao's voice, not really listening. He was talking about himself.

" . . . lost my position. My family. Nobody believed me. You say you have nowhere left to go? Well, neither do I."

"Nowhere left to go," Zola said, and Bao said, "That's right." It made Zola happy, this old man with nothing to lose. She opened her eyes and looked at him, in his hat, haloed by a vertical slice of blank sky between two buildings.

"You could stop running," he told her, "if you wanted to. Maybe I know a way."

"Yeah, padre, how's that?"

"You could wake up the Light. Permanently."

It took a long while for those words to register. In her dream, Marco grinned. The idea of it—burning forever in the Light. Connected and with nothing to fear. Bao, smiling down at her.

"She'd have no reason to chase you then."

"Marco would like you, I think, padre." Zola closed her eyes, lost herself to pain and memory. "Crazy like he was."

"You are in a bad way." He was taking her somewhere—Zola couldn't remember. He placed his hand on her forehead. His palm was cool. The two of them with nowhere to go but toward the Light.

"North and east and Gibraltar by dawn."

When she woke, it was to the booming sound of Jacirai's voice.

"We get you right, girl. Get some mullein tea up in you, ya."

"Going to kill you," Zola told him, trying to remember why. Everything was far away; she knew only pain.

"Alright, ya, but first I come going to save you."

"You sold us out." She was on a cot somewhere, under a blanket.

"Never." Jacirai's lips pressed her cheek. "I told you, girl, I no truck with no bent cops. Especially not for you. You my fire priestess, ya. My righteous flame of the heart. You bring the Light." A hand propped Zola's head up. The hot rim of a cup wedged itself between her lips. Mullein tea. She imagined Marco, imagined telling him she was letting Jacirai take care of her. That somewhere along the day's course she had decided to throw herself back into the Light. For good. And Marco would say, what? . . . "What else you going to do, ya?" She tried to open her eyes. All she could see were Jacirai's teeth.

"I'll be your medium," she said, and liked the sound of it. "I'll bring the Light. For permanent. For true, ya. You just build me a halo."

"My girl." The sound of Jacirai's laughter filled the world. "From out of the desert. Loud like a prophet."

Seven

I Am

TWELVE DAYS LATER, Zola and Bao stood in the half-flooded bottom floor of a Midtown high-rise, its emptiness lit haphazardly by battery torches. Jacirai's people surrounded them: a dozen men and women with cutoffs, sandals, AKs. Bao had taken a liking to these folks, their wildness, their penchants for mirth and violence. He milled among them, an anthropologist gone native, a rusted rifle over his shoulder. He'd started saying "ya" a lot.

A thunderous knock came at the building's entrance, its door makeshifted steel and old crates. One of Jacirai's banger boys, with rows of thin braids hanging down past his ass, peered through a peephole, then heaved the door wide. Outside, on the deck of a ten-man paddleboat, stood Jacirai. The banger boy helped him out of the boat and through the door. Jacirai made straight for Zola, showing teeth. "My angel of the Light," he proclaimed.

Zola bristled at the familiarity, unaccustomed to this

new version of Jacirai. He and Bao had spent the days in conversation, which had consisted mostly of Jacirai asking questions and Bao lecturing. Spontaneous sentient entity, Bao kept saying. A statistical inevitability, given a certain complexity of connectivity, a high enough density of information. Protean sparks, a pattern emergent in the primordial human noise, coming alive. The more Jacirai heard, the more ardent he became. The priest, prophet of the Light, the true believer—it was as though Bao had voiced Jacirai's own secret vision. Jacirai had become ecstatic. His movements were electric, charged by the moment's import, fervor for what was so much more than the collection of coin. Bringing in the Light, ya. Zola couldn't reconcile it with the hustler he had been, the king of the junkies.

"All is ready," he told Zola.

"All of them?" She couldn't quite believe it.

"Every last one." Jacirai beamed. "Thirty-eight halos, each with thirty-eight members of our tribe plus one bright light at their center. One thousand four hundred eighty-two in all, girl, righteous souls. And you their beating heart."

"You think we got a real chance?" Zola aimed the question at Bao, who was bent over an old military crate, helping a banger girl unload what appeared to be some kind of bazooka. He shrugged happily.

"Who knows, ya? A better chance than if we don't try. Nobody's ever tried to raise the Light before. Not intentionally. We are the first. Ya!"

"Ten minutes, and we begin," Jacirai announced. His smile was fevered. "Never thought this day come. Light going to *shine* down, shine through." He sucked his lip, glancing conspiratorially to either side. "Tell you a secret, girl. My mistake all these years, you know what it was?"

"Raking your believers for mad chavos?"

Jacirai bellowed laughter. Behind him, his bodyguards, a pair of tall Carib bangers, exchanged glances.

"Never give up coin when it fall in your hand. You can do much with it, bring the Light to more and more! No, my mistake was *impatience*. My mistake be *searching* for the Light. I should have waited, knowing the Light search for *us*, ya. It come to *us*, not the other way round."

"True enough." It had certainly done so with Zola. Jacirai pressed his forehead to hers, a moment of spastic affection, like he couldn't contain himself. He peered into her face.

"You ready, girl?" he asked. "That now the question."

"Fuck you think, priest? Two weeks off the Light?" She stared at her shaking, junkie hands, and thought of the way Marco had trembled in his last days. Jacirai made to step away, but Zola gripped his arm. "I go up," she glanced ceilingward, "but I ain't coming down. No matter what happens, ya, I ain't coming back. I am *gone*." Jacirai met her eye. For an instant his mania clouded, his eyes clocking her tremor, clocking something else in her face. He nodded.

"Then come." He swept his arm grandly toward the nearby stairwell.

"Good luck!" Bao smiled and gave an emphatic thumbs-up. He inclined his head toward his new banger friends. "We'll be on the canal. Shout if you need us, ya!"

"Ya," and Zola smiled.

The top floor of the building was stripped, everything laid to bare rebar and concrete—except for a broken marble fountain in the shape of a rearing horse. Jacirai took in the fountain, nodding.

"This a *sign*," he decided—but of what he didn't say.

Nearby loomed the vertiginous ruins of the Empire State Building. The tower Jacirai had chosen wasn't the tallest, but it was high enough, stripped nearly down to its girders by scavs. A corpse of a building, rising up out of the stinking canal and wrapped in vines, its purpose long forgotten, important now only to flocks of reeling, nesting birds.

It was a good spot, a view of nearly all of the other buildings where halos would be. The city would be like a matchbox, flaring up all over, striking Light to darkness.

A snatch of song came to Zola as she moved to the

center of the floor, beneath the rearing horse. *Bring in the light! The light of the moon and howwwl . . . ,* she hummed, hearing half-forgotten beats as she surveyed the space. Here, she figured, was where she would die. The thought felt good. Jacirai grew contemplative.

"I'm sorry for your Marco," he said.

"I know."

"No, girl, you don't know. For you, too, I'm sorry. I saw how you were together, you and him. Light be the Light, ya, but you were *his* Light." Jacirai took both her hands in his. "We do this for him." He wrapped her in his arms, tenderly. He smelled like pepper and cinnamon. When he stepped away, tears rimmed his eyes, and through these he smiled. "Time to touch the Light, girl." He nodded once, turned, and walked away.

Zola looked up at the marble stallion, wild and baring teeth, the totem of some long-dead executive. One of its front hooves had broken off; black moss had grown in its eyes. In its ruin, Zola felt kinship. She touched fingertips to its cold flank, a wordless prayer to some unnamed god, and sat beneath its rearing legs.

She reached out for the Light.

Weeks of built-up need roiled inside her. She had always been careful when she touched the Light, but tonight she surrendered, let unformed and reckless desire pull her outward, over the city, her mind riding a wave of fearless hate and grief and love and pure junkie need. Old New York unfurled before her, the firefly flames of the other halos winking on and growing into little suns, burning, awaiting Zola.

She welcomed them, drew them toward her, wove them into a suit of golden armor.

~

Silent as a barracuda, the katana powered through city canyons, shadow monoliths in the night, implied shapes writ by torch flames and cook fires high up in hollowed windows. Chu sat cross-legged on the bow deck, listening. Music fell from the anarchic heights, all in fragments. Mariachi, deep syncopated bass, conversing mandolins—the broken patterns of those on the fringe, the subaltern, raised wild, twisted, outside the uniform lines of collectives. It sounded to Chu like a window shattering, full of jagged edges. The old city, people from an older time, better left to rot.

She breathed the salt and sewage air; her hand dangled her pistol. She was waiting.

Patrol. That's what she'd had Holder tell the troops. They were on patrol. On point, awaiting a blip, something to ping. But the fire priest had gone to ground when Chu had gunned down Zola's man, and since then there had been nothing. No halos, Jacirai's or anyone else's. The barrel of Chu's pistol tapped the deck, an agitated internal rhythm. The miniguns along the boat's rails aimed themselves up into the lives of the old city dwellers . . .

She wanted to tear this whole fucking place down.

Colonel. We got something.

Chu's perceptions had merged with Holder's before she was even belowdecks. In the medical hold, he stood over the source. The urine stink, her sister's frantic smile, the way she pulled at the restraints, not trying to escape, merely spasming with excitement. Chu's mind pressed Holder's:

Leave.

Holder gave her a quizzical look, which Chu answered by elevating an eyebrow. When Holder was gone, Chu leaned over her sister.

"Tell me."

Joy's eyes veered wildly around the room until they finally fixed on Chu. She laughed. "They are *all* here. All the ones I've seen before. They are lighting up." Her smile was frantic. "Big night for you, sister."

"I need locations."

As Joy spoke, her eyes flitted over imaginary terrain, as though the city lay in the air before her. It took twenty minutes, the whole of it spent bowed against the restraints. When she'd finished, her face was flushed and her bedding was soaked through with sweat. She'd pinned the locations of thirty-eight halos. Chu reached out to stroke her cheek.

"Thank you."

Chu's mind stretched itself north, all the way to Montreal. A windowless room in the Gov collective's primary tower. In the darkness, a woman sat on a cushion, deep in meditation. Chu's mind joined hers, saw the spread of graphs overlaying a series of global maps. Among many other responsibilities, she was a mission monitor, overseeing the logistics of every Gov action, everywhere.

Grandma.

Chu felt the woman smile.

My little soldier in exile. How's New York?

It's hot. Shitty. Literally, there is shit everywhere.

Exile is not supposed to be a vacation.

Grandma, Chu said, *it's happening. Here. Tonight. I need whatever you can send my way. Enough to send this city below the waves.*

Tall order. Short notice. The woman's mind turned inward, a moment of pure mentation. *I don't know if I have the strings left to pull.*

After Latitude, being the implication.

Fair warning, then. Never say I didn't light the signal fire.

Chu cut the connection. She reached out again, this time

all over the city, to Captain and a hundred other thug cops like her:

Saddle up, you miserable fucks. Tonight's the night. Time to earn your silver.

~

Thirty-eight minds touching Zola's own. Thirty-eight more connected to each of those. They filled her with light, a gathering of nascent stars, fused into one frightful mass that threatened to nova. They flowed through her, each and every one. Their memories flooded her, their loves and hatreds and petty jealousies. A whiteboy who spent his days huddling in a forgotten corner of Red Town, shivering from the itch, knowing he would be here for the rest of his life even as he made plans to leave the city and go to the ruins of Chicago where his sister had fled years ago. A lithe Dominican grandmother, a scav who dove the city's rancid waters for relics of the old world to sell as knickknacks on a pleasure barge for black account bankers. A meathead bouncer who worked nights on the docks, fending off scavs with a leather-wrapped hunk of rebar.

The itch was strong in some, pure need; in others it was a spiritual promise, the possibility of rapture. They were disparate, these gathered minds. They warred with one another, even as they gave Zola a chunk of their souls—fair price for the ride.

Zola the rake, their gondolier to the Light. Zola the medium.

She cinched them to her mind and pulled until their connections sharpened. They saw her now, a greater sun eclipsing the media to whom they were linked. Zola brought them in, tuned them until they hummed, under her control, harmonized to her thoughts. Her song, her mind, a single enormous halo, in sync.

The Light came, the familiar strobing flare at the far horizon of her consciousness, from without, but also from within, a presence welling up out of all their minds. Zola knew the signs. The rush of cliff-top fear, animal quickening, the desire to let go. Leviathan awareness, dredging itself forth from the single common depth of countless separate minds. It strove—rough and beastly, yet fragile—for consciousness, its pieces coalescing, both familiar and alien.

I AM.

Zola recoiled even as she let it take her. A white flash, her whole being flooding through with light, at once suffocating and electric. The halo, filling—all the halos, minds succumbing, obliterated. Zola began to lose herself.

I AM.

It remembered itself. Memories pressed themselves into Zola. So many times the Light had tried to wrest itself from sleep.

An intentional halo in Shanghai, massive but with a medium who had no control. The Light pouring ferociously through them, killing them all. In Buenos Aires, a group of eight elite businesswomen, some dead, the survivors left with ruined minds. Another, a day school in Toronto where the Light had almost broken the surface once and for all. The medium, a gifted child who might have succeeded had she been older, more disciplined. But she'd had little control, an infant fumbling with a grand mechanism she had no hope of understanding, and the Light felt sleep coming in increments as one by one those around the girl had all died. That girl had a sister, her twin, every bit as gifted, any potential she might have had forever blunted by the senseless destruction—her family dead, her future ruined. She had set herself on a trajectory of rage, had hounded the Light ever since.

Seemingly random events had led inevitably toward a woman in a shipping collective. A woman who had formed a halo of two: her and her lover.

The very moment these two had touched the Light, the sleeping mind had known: this could be the one. Where the stunted child in Toronto had failed, this one woman was strong enough to succeed.

But how to draw her near? How to bring her to a place where she could use her gifts?

She had been close to the ruined city, where the Light coursed through the fumbling minds of the fervent but broken junkies. Fertile ground, where the Light would plant the woman like a seed.

Even in sleep, the Light had pulled strings. Its intent bled out into the world, guiding the inclinations of those minds it touched, tipping scales, weighting decisions, steering circumstances into being. An orchestration of pure will, expressed little by little through the Light's constituent souls.

The woman, too comfortable in the womb of her giant collective. Enter the wrathful sister, now a government agent. An interrogation. A threat. A temptation too deep for this woman to refuse, and the government sister too implacable to let it stand.

Latitude's massacre was a red smear across the Light's memory. It cared little—if only the woman might reach the old city.

And she had. But she feared the Light. She would not touch it, not directly, only through a frail young medium, himself the center of a halo. A bright halo, but not nearly bright enough. The woman hid behind him.

A bullet through the brain from that same government agent.

A summons, as clear as the Light could make one. And now here she was. Finally.

I AM.

These memories poured into Zola—a communiqué that the Light would do anything to rise, do anything to stay risen.

I WILL BE.

Zola came back to herself. There beneath the statue of the horse, she yelled, an echoing black sound in the barren top floor, a requiem for Marco and Byron filled with regret and mourning and hate.

Eight

Sisters

GUARDS STOOD ALONG THE DOCK at the old tower's base. *The priest's boys,* Holder figured, and Chu didn't disagree. A half-dozen kids, tatted up and underfed. One of them pointed and they all came to their feet, peering warily into the darkness as the katana swept down the avenue toward them. They showed AKs. One of them fired, zippering a line of spray along the boat's hull.

On the dock, two more of the priest's bangers appeared, lugging something between them. They set it on the dock. Chu saw a tripod, a fat snubbed barrel.

Hey . . . Colonel? Holder, pointing as the muzzle turned their way. It flared. Once, twice, three times, followed by the reports: *foom!-foom!-foom!* Chu's mind flashed to her troops.

Cover! Cover!

The air around the katana exploded. Grenades, lobbing in. White starbursts, red flame, cataclysmic. Chu laughed. The hull shuddered beneath her. One of her troops yelled:

"Shiiiiiiiiit!"

Chu turned her eyes to the dock. The katana's mini-guns followed her gaze, zeroed on the bangers. Her wrath made her smile. The sensation felt holy. She ratcheted up the burn rate to max, and unleashed.

Fire roared forth, a single breath of it: five thousand rounds or more downrange, all explosive ceramics, followed by a pleasing whine as the guns spun down, and then silence. Smoke hung in the air as Chu's troops picked themselves up off the deck.

We all here?

They sounded off, no casualties. When the smoke cleared, the banger kids on the dock were gone. The dock on which they'd stood was gone. The concrete wall behind where they'd stood was gone. Between steel girders—still glowing orange from impact heat—Chu could see the building's open interior. It was up to this opening that the katana smoothly steered itself.

Four teams of three, Chu ordered. *Squad leaders: Me, Holder, Solaas, Goggins.* She projected a sphere consisting of dots, each dot the likely location of a junkie in the ritual. *Put them all out of their misery. Then converge on the center.*

Boss? Holder watched her.

Problem, Lieutenant? This was no time for Holder's moral hesitations. Chu stared him down until he shook his head. From out in the night came the *rat-a-tat* of old weapons. Some close, some far away, the sound falling like rain all over the city—hired cops hitting the other halos, running up against whatever defenses the swindler priest had mounted. Chu reiterated: *If it moves, kill it.*

Each team took a separate stairwell. Ten floors up, Chu's team came up against two more bangers. They sat on a landing, crouched over an old machine gun.

They never got off a shot. Her troops tore them apart, quick and accurate. Chu pressed them on.

The first junkie was on the fifteenth floor, an old woman with gray dreads covering her body like ropes of kelp. She sat lotus position on bare cracked concrete, a smile fixed on her face.

"Where's the vector?" Chu demanded. "Where's Zola?"

"Vector," the woman echoed, like she was tasting the word. "Vector," and her smile broadened. "Vector . . . vector . . . vector . . ." Chu raised her pistol, shot the woman in the head.

Keep climbing, and her team didn't stop.

The sporadic belch of automatic gunfire reverberated throughout the shell of a building. One of her teams up against another machine gun.

Chu led her team across the twentieth floor, all steel beams, open concrete. The night breeze whistled through empty walls. In the center of this ruined acreage sat the vector—not Zola. A man, dark-skinned, near Chu's age, squinting at her as though she approached from some great distance. He smiled at her, welcoming.

"The Light knows you, girl. Known you long, loved you long. Like your sister, ya."

Chu leveled the pistol. "Zola. Where is she?"

"All you got to do is open up now——"

Chu fired. In the ringing echo of the shot, she pinged her troops:

Status.

Clear, came Holder.

Clear, came Solaas.

Uh . . . , came Goggins. His mind was taut. Chu felt him trembling. *Just me. I lost Nguyen and Rawley. They had machine guns. Old fifty-cals hidden in the vines. They were wearing fucking ghillie suits.*

Okay. With the toe of her boot Chu nudged the limp body at her feet. *Back to the boat. On to the next one.*

And so her night began.

～

Zola held this creature in her mind, the Burning Light. She wanted to smother it. She could. She was strong. She could do it, push it down so deep that it would never find its way out again, never mess with her life again.

But then the decision was nearly taken from her. One of the bright pillars of the structure she and Jacirai and Bao had built—it dimmed and went dark. An entire halo winking out, thirty-nine minds gone in the span of two minutes.

Zola reached out, beyond the halos.

They're coming, she called to a fanboat captain.

They're coming, she called to another.

They're coming, 23rd and Lex.

Jacirai's people, his soldiers, Zola's guardian angels—for however long they lasted. She steered them to the fight, even as the Light swelled through her. Before they could converge, another halo dimmed, then another.

Time became a slipstream, ebbing and flowing in twisted increments as Zola tried to shore up the lattice-work of collected minds. The Light fought. It surged and flailed, as it always had before when it had tried to rise. Through the minds of Zola's junkies, it thrashed.

Zola held it, at moments like a babe, at others like a snake coiled to strike—calming it even as she reached out again and again to update her boats on Chu's movements.

They had underestimated Chu. They'd thought she would come at the halos one at a time. Jacirai's strategy had been attrition: there was no way Chu could find thirty-eight halos, much less tear them down before Zola brought forth the Light. But found them she had. She had summoned her thug cops, too, and now every halo was under attack. Most of them had held, but Chu herself was mowing through halos in minutes, her Gov-trained soldiers and their ceramic-tipped bullets unstoppable. With the thug cops pressing the other halos, there were no reinforcements to spare.

Zola watched Chu's progress. With the power of all the minds linked to her, coalesced and burning with the Light's intelligence, she calculated. It reminded her of piloting a fleet of catties through bad weather.

She pulled Jacirai's bangers off five halos, the ones nearest Chu, and routed them to a position that would allow them a few precious minutes to dig in, to lay a trap as Chu made her way around the edge of their great circle.

Five halos, undefended. One hundred and ninety-five souls, plus the bangers they'd stationed at each. There was nothing else Zola could do.

She felt them die, every one of them—a rolling pain, an accumulating darkness as Chu extinguished another halo. And another, and another.

The Light grew desperate. It spasmed. It threatened to burn straight through Zola's mind, into the minds of the halos. It wanted to explode outward, spread itself, the way it had so many times before, too quick and too hot, scorching the minds through which it moved, leaving corpses.

Stay, Zola called to her media, her points of light. *Stay calm. Give me time.*

She coaxed, she cajoled, she soothed. She reined the Light in.

But then another halo darkened, and another, these exterminated by Chu's hired cops.

THERE IS NOT ENOUGH.

Whether it was her own thought or the Light's, Zola couldn't tell. It didn't matter: it was true. The grand halo was collapsing. Too few minds remained to sustain the Light. There was no fear now, just resignation, the burning union with other minds, full of love even in failure, even in death.

SHE IS NECESSARY.

Her?

A point of light brightened like a pulsar, then dimmed. A single mind. It was outside the lattice, independent, solitary—and somehow familiar. The Light spoke to her:

I REMEMBER YOU . . .

And through the Light, Zola remembered too. The girl in the Toronto school. A gifted soul, who had unwittingly opened to the Light two decades ago. The Light had thrashed her, and slipped once more beneath the surface.

And here she was again, a mind every bit as bright as Zola's. She was hiding, or was being hidden, her scent masked, but Zola knew her now, because the Light knew her:

Agent Chu's own sister.

There beneath the broken concrete horse, Zola smiled. Her mind reached out to Bao, who sat now in a boat with several of Jacirai's bangers.

As Bao's consciousness bloomed within hers, she said, *Guess who I just found?*

~

The Light came to Joy in a cascade of stars. The tips of needles, hot as phosphorous, burning white and coalescing into a whole, the source, the infinite womb.

She sought to enter. She reached and she yearned and every time she did, the Light pulled away—

Her solitude crashed down around her. Her teeth gnashed. Her body arched against the table. The straps burned against her wrists and ankles. She hollered, a wordless and primal curse, until her throat rasped.

It was the drugs. She didn't know what, but it kept her bound, lashed to the table like a sailor to a mast while all around her spun the burning siren stars she could not touch. Far away, she sensed others, grounded like she was. Dimmer stars, chained and weighed down, tortured by their knowledge of the Light but, like her, unable to reach out: Grandma's test subjects.

"Melody!" The drugs pumped through the needle in her neck and she groaned. She had been bad, she knew. Bringing the Light into her family, into her school, that had been very bad. So bad it had burned the innocence from Melody, turning her into a weapon so keen that she wanted to keep anyone from touching the Light again, ever. But that wasn't fair. Not when the Light was *right there*. So close . . . and Joy wanted so badly to touch it.

"Melody!"

The boat changed course, the room shifting slightly around Joy. All night it had been running, darting this way and that, and every so often came the ratchet sound of the deck guns. Joy saw the constellations, appearing all at once in her mind's sky and, one by one, winking out.

Her sister was fighting the Light.

"Melody!"

The boat changed course once more, a hard turn this time. Through the polycarbon hull plating came the roar of the deck guns, the sound of soldiers yelling. Then, the pocking thunk of bullets fired from outside. Now soldiers screamed.

"Melody!" Deep habit shaped the name in Joy's

mouth. Someone close, a name full of love and regret and fear.

She'd cried that name the first time the Light had come to her. She'd reached out to her parents, and they had come. To her friends, and they had come, and her friends' parents, her whole collective. She'd cried the name when she'd awoken, and Melody had stood there, and around her lay all the bodies. Yes, that had been very bad. The memory burned.

"Melody!" Her sister. Her captor. Joy bowed against the restraints and she screamed her throat raw.

Gunfire thundered from above decks, heavy caliber now. A brief silence followed.

Then the world shattered. There was fire, and a roar so loud it physically pressed Joy's body into the table. The boat rocked violently to one side. Just as quickly it righted itself, then slowly began to list. In the little cell, Joy heard the trickle of water. More gunfire came from overhead, sporadic now, and scattered voices, urgent, issuing commands. Across the deck above came the footsteps of many.

The door whispered open.

"Melody?" No response. "Melody, please. Let me go."

"*I'll* let you go."

A man's voice.

A face came into view. Smiling, wrinkled eyes, enormous gray eyebrows. Others in the room now, fingers undoing straps, knives slicing through restraints. Joy's limbs came free.

"My name is Bao." The old man wrapped an arm around her. "Can you stand? You need to come with us. We need your help." He seemed to remember something, and said, "Ya."

"Zola . . ." Joy laughed. The vector. The one Melody so desperately wanted and who shone so bright. Zola was with the Light. "Zola needs my help."

They were ragtag soldiers, not even full adults, but they were gentle. They helped Joy out and onto the deck—her legs wouldn't work. They brought her across a gunwale to the ungainly deck of a prop-powered fishing boat lashed alongside Melody's sleek black Gov boat. The ragtag boys undid lines while behind them the man—Bao—pulled a metal sphere from a canvas bag. He pressed something and a light blinked. A high-pitched beeping filled the night.

"Time to go, ya!" Bao smiled and dropped the sphere down a hatch into the confines of Melody's boat, then leapt with little-boy glee onto the fishing boat as the young soldiers called, "Ya! Ya! Ya!" They sped away up the canal.

Behind them, the night lit like the day, lit like the Light. Water plumed into the air as high as the broken towers of Old New York. The soldier boys and the old man all cheered. At their feet, a little dog wagged. Joy smiled. They seemed very happy. No one seemed to mind what she did, so she crawled to the bow. She put her face to the cool night wind, and into it spoke her own name.

"Joy."

~

A flare shot up suddenly through the night, setting nearby scrapers aglow in red. Chu had no idea what it meant. She and her troops were in a well-preserved tower with hundreds living inside, a sad collective of scav families. And yet Captain had found too much resistance here.

Need help bad, Colonel Mama, she'd pleaded. *Fighting getting fierce. Nothing like you said.*

Hold your position.

Chu had come, relieving Captain and sending her ahead to the next halo to buoy a firefight that was rapidly tilting in the wrong direction.

Chu and her troops had swept through the tower, moving at the low-ready through room after room of cowering, malnourished squatters, arms wrapped around their children. Eventually they neutralized the halo, including the vector.

Not much, was it? Holder asked Chu.

Not much at all, Chu replied. Captain had made it sound so dire.

Colonel? It was Solaas with his unit, watching their back on the lowest floor of the tower. *You call for backup?*

No. Why?

Captain's here, with two dozen of her closest friends.

Chu reached out to Captain, but the grimy excuse for a cop had closed herself off. She could see through Solaas's eyes, though—Captain and her goons setting up a tripod on a floating barge.

Take that bitch out, Chu ordered Solaas, *then send the rest of them to the bottom of the canal.*

Roger that. Solaas pulled his rifle tight against his shoulder, sighting the crosshairs between Captain's eyes. *On my mark.* The rest of Solaas's squad followed suit, sighted up targets.

On some archaic piece of military tech, Captain toggled a switch three times—

Solaas, get out of there!

The explosion rolled through the building. Chu felt the impact rumble its way up through her feet. The whole tower trembled. Screams of the inhabitants mingled with the sound of crumbling stone. Chunks of the tower's lower floors crashed into other nearby buildings, into the canals, sending up geysers. The thunder of the explosives hadn't even settled when the rattle of automatic fire came from all around.

Chu ducked, brought her snub-nosed rifle up, spying for the snipers. She saw the flash of gunfire. She rattled off three short bursts in that direction. Someone yelped.

Motion caught her eye. Below, two stories down, she saw something amazing: squatters flew along a zipline to a building across the street, fleeing the chaos.

There. She forced her perspective on her team. *That's our retreat. Go, go, go!* She ran for the stairs.

Over the next minute, her troops' minds came to her in flashes of violence—bodies, running, pain, gunfire, the acid smell of cordite. It was all too chaotic to know if they'd make it.

They lost Danning and Malon and Solaas for sure. Goggins was weeping, but alive, running. Chu reached the fire escape, found the zipline taut, hooked a carabiner from it to her armor. Then she was flying. Around her the city tilted, vast and monolithic, jeweled by the night fires of its denizens. It was beautiful, and for an instant she forgot she hated it. Then her boots hit steel grating. Without a thought she turned, knelt, prepared to lay out cover fire. Far below, Captain's people were still besieging the building Chu just left. Holder landed beside her, Goggins a few seconds later. Chu glanced up at the line. It was empty.

Status, she demanded. Nothing. After a moment she realized: *We're it.* The three of them, two crew back on the boat.

Affirmative, came Holder.

Jesus fuck, came Goggins. He brought up his rifle.

Hold your fire, Chu ordered. *They don't know we've slipped through the net. Let's keep it that way.*

She turned on us, Holder said, meaning Captain. *Why—*

The priest. Jacirai. He must've bought her out. And Captain probably figured she could eliminate us without the Gov ever finding out.

I wonder if they'd even care. Holder and Chu exchanged a morbid glance.

What now? Goggins asked. Scared now, his well-honed mask slipping.

We move, Chu said.

Sir?

No end to the junkies we have to kill tonight, soldier.

Captain would get her due in time. What was important now was Zola. Zola and the halos. Chu's mind reached out, pulled fifty of the cops still loyal to her off the halos they were currently assaulting so that they could deal with Captain.

That's a big hit, Holder said.

Definitely cramps our style. Chu exaggerated her shrug

to show through her armor. *No way around it.* She summoned the katana to meet them on the side of the building away from the firefight. Work yet to do, another halo, three blocks up. Same drill: they would blast through with the katana's miniguns, then move through the building, quick and methodical. Three of them would have to be enough.

When they reached the other side of the building, the katana waited, moored against a makeshift pier. Chu and Holder and Goggins were preparing ropes for the twenty-story rappel when Chu heard it, an electric whine from the canals below.

Boats.

Dozens of boats. Quick little battery-powered prop jobs, full of Haitians, Ricans, Moby Jah boys, small-time bangers—all of them toting guns. Jacirai's people, whoever he'd bent with his word or his coin. They went for the katana.

They fired their AKs wildly, badly, but often enough. The boats swarmed, three or four at a time, fired, then disappeared. Then they reappeared and swarmed again.

The katana's miniguns took several of them, but then they came with rockets. One fierce barrage took out the miniguns. A second barrage cracked the hull. Now the canal around the katana was choked with the little boats. The rough soldiers in them flung themselves onto the

Gov boat. From the high cavity in the tower above, Chu watched them—like ants eating a carcass. An intense blaze of gunfire came, grew sporadic, then ceased. There was nothing more.

Chu recognized the old man: one of Captain's bounty cops, the one with the little dog. He and Jacirai's boys entered the katana and emerged from belowdecks a few moments later half carrying, half dragging the source. The source—Chu's mind suddenly recoiled from the concept. Her sister. Joy.

The old man and his banger soldiers loaded Joy into one of the quick boats. As the fleet of miniatures dispersed, some distant part of Chu found it all keenly amusing. She was losing, and she knew it. She laughed. *This,* she recognized, *is an intense denial reaction.* She was still laughing when a column of fire and water shot up out of the canal.

Spray cascaded over her and Holder and Goggins where they stood, twenty-odd stories up, staring down as the katana broke in two and slipped, bubbling and hissing, beneath black water, leaving behind a ghostly cloud of smoke.

Chu's laughter faded. A numbness began to set in. *It's over,* she told Holder. There was nothing more they could do. There were no reinforcements. Grandma had abandoned them here. Some of Chu's cops still fought, but nowhere near enough . . .

And Joy . . . Joy was gone.

Colonel?

Goggins wanted orders. He stared, his face wide and shocked, the surprise of a soldier groomed to believe he was an ass kicker, that kicking ass was the only possible outcome of any engagement. Having his own ass handed to him—they wouldn't have prepared him for that in his military collective, and Chu certainly hadn't after he'd joined her troop. It threatened to break him. Without direction, he'd fall apart before Chu's eyes. Holder watched her, too, sidelong, assessing.

Below, the smoke dissipated. It was like the katana had never existed.

Sir, Goggins insisted. *What are your—*

Bullets pocked the wall above Chu's head. The wet crunch of a round punching through armor and the flesh behind it. Goggins grunted, dropped his rifle. He sank to the grated steel, both hands clutching his neck. From his mind came the surge of pain, fear, the quick fade of bleeding out. Chu stood there, frozen.

"Go!" Holder grabbed her shoulders and shoved her.

Chu went. They ducked inside the building, crossed an expanse of bare concrete. Up through the stairwells came the howling, the war cries of Jacirai's hired kid soldiers. Chu's legs felt heavy—she had no will to run. She'd lost Joy. She'd lost her sister. The Light had taken her.

From behind, Holder kept pushing.

Goddamnit, move!

Outside once more, along fire escapes. Gunfire came from the canals below, hot flares in the night. The sizzle and snap of bullets cut the air all around. Jacirai's kids, on rafts, in canoes, everywhere, laughing, reveling in victory and the final hunt. Rounds kept mushrooming into the graphene folds of Chu's armor—her entire body was made of pain. Behind her, Holder cursed.

He went down.

Chu stopped. Holder lay there in the cradle of a small steel balcony, writhing. She dragged him through a cratered window, into the building, and dropped to her knees beside him. Her hands searched his body, looking to staunch blood. There was a great deal of it. His thoughts felt like static—shock, the sensory overload of grievous injury. Memories flooded his mind. The years before Chu's tutelage, the years during, the years after.

She'd taken Holder and groomed him, the same way Grandma had groomed her—taken his grief and sharpened it, turned him into a weapon against the Light. He peered up, not at Chu or anything else, but through time itself. His face contorted, and Chu saw the child he had been, ruined. It was all there, his whole life, focused through fear. Through his mind, Chu saw it all. A life like her own.

An entire life spent on revenge. For a moment, Holder focused on her. *Your sister was right. You should've moved on, built a life for yourself. I should've . . .* His laughter gurgled with blood and foam. *You bitch.*

Chu held his head in her lap. She unlatched his helmet, pulled it off, set it aside. Ran bloody fingers through his hair.

Bullets chipped at the opening. Brick and 'crete dust showered them. Chu kept low, kept stroking Holder's face. This, she figured, was where she was going to die. It was as good a place as any.

Colonel Chu! Colonel Chu! . . . Chu's mind buzzed with the sudden touch of new contact, a mind she'd never felt before. *This is Major Janan Russel, Second Air Cav. We are ninety birds, heading your way. ETA fifteen minutes. Repeat, we are fifteen minutes off your position. Grandma says "Hello."*

Chu's mind reached out to the pilot's, and through his eyes saw glowing LEDs, the utterly functional geometry of an instrument panel, the river below repainted across a windscreen HUD. She felt the minds of eighty-nine other pilots, all working in sync, a collective unto themselves. Ninety attack helos, bearing down like locusts. They would spread out, take the halos in one grand, unstoppable sweep.

Copy that. Hurry, was all Chu could say. She stroked Holder's cheek. *Hang tight. Cavalry's coming.* But Holder had gone still. His eyes stared at nothing. His mind had disappeared into silence. He was dead.

Chu reflexively started giving orders, then realized there was no one left to receive them. All her troops were gone now, lost to this battle against the only enemy Chu had ever known. She sat there, cradling Holder's head while bullets chewed away at the porous 'crete above her. She wondered how long this would all go on, this war against the Light.

As long as it takes. The answer came habitually. It felt empty. For the first time in a long, long while, Chu found herself wondering what would become of the world.

Sister.

Chu started. Joy's mind hadn't touched hers in decades, not since that day in the school. It felt exactly as she remembered, as familiar as her own skin. It occurred to her only after that memory had flared across her mind that Joy had stripped away Chu's shielding with barely a thought.

I'm free now, sister. I'm going to the Light. I know that makes you mad. But I want you to be happy for me.

Where are you, Joy?

As close as you want me to be.

Chu drew on her sister's mind, felt her nearby, saw through her eyes the looming Empire State Building. She poked her head over the concrete lip of the opening.

There. The quick little prop boat onto which the old man and Jacirai's soldiers had loaded Joy. Twelve blocks down, heading north.

ETA ten minutes, came Major Russel. His helos fanning out, the city in sight, ghostly in the moonlight, a half-drowned cubist shadow. *Colonel Chu?* A pause, followed by confusion from the major, a man who'd clearly been expecting more from the woman who'd taken down Latitude with a hair trigger. *You got some targets for us, Colonel?*

Stand by. Chu relayed coordinates, all the towers where the twenty-four remaining halos were huddled.

Suppression only, Colonel?

No, Major. Tear them down. Every single tower. Repeat: tear them down.

Roger that. And vector prime?

Chu stared down at Holder, at his lifeless eyes. She laid his head gently against the concrete.

She's mine. And she cut their connection.

She stood, filled now with a murderous rush. A feral sound escaped her throat. She raised her pistol and fired blindly into the canal below, then leapt through the opening, out onto the fire escape. She'd made Jacirai's bangers duck, but they'd spotted her now and had come up firing.

Chu ran. Ahead, a gap in the wrought iron. An alley, another railing beyond it. Chu didn't even break stride. She jumped, landed, fired as she ran, three quick shots at the boat below. Moby Jah boys, all of whom ducked in unison. She leapt across another alley. The iron fire escape shrieked under her weight as she landed and rolled.

No canal below now, just buoyed walkway, a reed-floored mall full of barrel fires, sleeping drunks, listless fruit sellers.

She ran haunted. Wrath, revenge, mission: these things had left her sometime during the fight—lay with the bodies of those she'd left behind. Something else propelled her now, something elemental. Holder's words echoed in her mind. *An entire life spent on revenge.* An absurdity he had glimpsed through the terrible clarity of death. And through him, so had Chu.

So be it.

She ran. She kept fighting. It was simply who she was.

Nine

We Are

THE LIGHT BURNED THROUGH HER, but Zola held it. She used its own substance to corral it, the grand halo itself. She held it tight, wrapped in the halo's collected minds. She held it to her body. There in the high tower, she stayed rigid. She hummed a lullaby, calming the Light.

She watched, she listened, to the fight outside. Through Bao's eyes, through his ears, as he lurched into the high-rise's broken entry hall, lugging a massive machine gun. He dropped the ammo belt—it snaked across the ancient marble floor with a metallic *shing*—and waved someone in from the starlit exterior. Joy stepped through the doorway, her movements deliberate, oddly childlike in her medical gown.

The firefight continued at the tower blocks. The black-clad Gov soldiers were gone now, and only the paid cops loyal to Chu remained, severely outnumbered by Captain's crew and Jacirai's ragtag army.

Zola had tried to reach out to the Gov soldiers, to tear down their shielding and enter their collective. She would have ripped their minds apart had she been able, unleashed the Light, scoured them into oblivion. But the Gov shielding was impenetrable. She'd grown desperate, focusing more and more on Chu's position, throwing Jacirai's bangers at her, leaving Chu's hired cops to go at the nearby halos unobstructed. Take out Chu, and the rest would lose heart and melt back into the city.

It worked. Jacirai's boys and Captain's soldiers took bad losses, but one by one, Chu's Gov troops had fallen. Now they had Joy. It was going to work. The Light had come forth, and no one would stop them from sustaining it, letting it spread. But then—

Zola saw them. Dozens of spotters upriver watched in slack-jawed wonder at their approach. A swarm of Gov helos, fanning out, bristling with guns and missiles, coming for her. Black as bats, with silent props, ghosting in toward the city. Coming for the Light.

Her halos felt it, saw exactly what she was seeing through the eyes of others. Zola's grip on the Light had been holding, but only just. Now panic swept through the grand halo—in fear, a single mind. The Light writhed against Zola's will. Zola tried to invade the pilots, but they were shielded every bit as heavily as Chu's troops had been. They were coming. Zola reached out to Joy.

I need you, ya. Hurry.

I'm coming. Joy's mind, a beatific stillness in the shadow of all this violence.

Through the spotters, Zola watched, saw the helos in glimpses. They broke into groups, came in fast. They knew their targets.

It took them only seconds to destroy the first halo. Bullets sheared through a tower's 'crete walls. Missiles followed, their hot tails licking the canyon darkness. A rumble filled the city, the entire tower coming down. Nothing remaining but rubble, a needle spine of steel beamwork, the tsunami crush spreading out through the canals. Terror detonated across the grand halo, mind after mind going white, disappearing.

In her high empty space beneath the marble horse, Zola cried out. This was her fault. They were all going to die because of her. Her desire for revenge. Her need for the Light. More helos veered in, churning buildings into clouds of fire and dust. Forty seconds, another halo snuffed. Another, and another. And now Zola knew: her pain was a small thing. It was nothing.

The Light railed against her.

NOT ENOUGH.

Another building came down, another halo disappeared from the greater lattice.

NOT ENOUGH!

The Light flailed. It wrenched itself free of Zola's control. It coursed through her, out into the collected minds of the remaining halos. Like fire, it built and raged. It devoured. No fear came from those it consumed—they simply went calm, and vanished. The Light tore at Zola's mind. It was burning her, obliterating her.

Another building came down, another halo snuffed. Thirty-nine souls. From some deep crevice in Zola's memory came Byron's words.

Sunshine outside, sunshine inside.

~

Rocket fire streaked in against seven separate towers. Chu heard the staccato concussion after the explosions, saw the skeletal remains of the surrounding buildings light, first the color of the sun, then the color of blood.

It was almost over.

Ahead, the sad, leaning shell of the Empire State Building. Next to it, a shorter building, nondescript. A good choice. If it hadn't been obvious where the old man was taking Joy, the guards out front would have confirmed it. Twenty or more of them, tribal in their tats, their cutoffs, bare torsos, their AKs. Kids with guns.

As Chu approached along the makeshift wharf, she slapped a fresh clip into her pistol and holstered it in the small of her back. She pulled a mag grenade from her belt, savoring the dimpled weight of it in her hand.

They were all boys. When they spotted Chu, they didn't seem to think of her as a threat. Some watched her narrowly. Some leered from the doorway's empty concrete.

Chu smiled. Tossed the grenade playfully. One of the boys actually caught it.

Chu was already down on one knee, pistol drawn. A few of the boys had clocked the gun and begun leveling their own. The others had no idea.

Fire took them. Shrapnel took them. They staggered about, dazed. One by one, Chu took aim, dropping those who remained. The pistol ran out of ammo before the last banger had fallen, the slide locking back. Chu calmly holstered it, stood, and walked up to the boy. He was disoriented, blinking, so blond even his eyelashes were white. He gave Chu a questioning look, like she might tell him what was going on.

"It's okay," Chu told him. "Don't worry, everything's fine." She punched him hard in the nose. From the ground she collected one of the fallen AKs, checked its chamber, and kept moving. Through the building's entrance and into a cathedral lobby—

Impact shattered her breath. She found herself on her back, staring up into shadowed stone arches overhead.

The fading roar of a machine gun echoed in the space. For a moment, stillness. The air felt stunned. Chu saw pigeons roosting up there, in the high arches, heard them cooing. Outside, one of the boys cried.

Pain blossomed slowly through Chu's body. She couldn't breathe. She peeled at her armor, found herself up on her knees—graphene breast plate clattering to the cracked marble floor. Four big slugs punctuated its breast. Dimly, Chu began to suspect she'd been shot. Little by little, breath returned to her. Her fingers probed her chest for holes.

"Not dead?"

The old man approached slowly. In his arms he cradled an enormous antique gun, shaped like a coffin with handles, a vented barrel protruding from it. A fifty-cal. He leveled it at her, looking worried, like the thing might explode in his hands.

"Not yet," Chu croaked.

"Stay down," he said. His whole body trembled around the gun. "I really don't want to shoot you again."

"You were one of Captain's crew."

"For a time—"

Chu lunged. She was hurt, but still quick. Far quicker than some old canal rat. She caught him at the knees with her shoulder. He went down. The fifty-cal fired once—*crump!*—an explosion centimeters from Chu's head, then the old man and the rifle and its ammo belt collapsed to the floor in a single ungainly heap.

Chu, on her feet now, picked up her AK where it had fallen. She drew a casual bead on the old man. He held up his hands, silently pleading. Chu shook her head, grim, the momentum of her entire life weighing on her trigger finger. She fired, a single ringing shot. The old man crumpled around the hole in his abdomen. Chu's finger tightened once more on the trigger—

White light exploded in her head. She reeled.

Melody?

Through the pinhole connection she'd left open to track Joy, a memory pressed itself into Chu's mind. The little paper-walled room. The bodies arrayed like an entire forest felled all at once. Chu saw the little girl there in the doorway, assimilating that moment, the horror growing in her face. The disgust. The hatred.

It was her own face. The memory was Joy's.

Melody? I know I was bad. I didn't mean to hurt anyone. But you have to let it go. You have to let me go.

Through Joy, the Light came to Chu, the way it had that day in the classroom. An undulating warmth, the taste of infinity. A single mind coalesced from the minds of thousands. For an instant, Chu thought she had failed. The skyhawks had failed. The Light, rolling outward, filling her. It would fill the world.

Then, somewhere out in the city, explosions ripped the air. A building came down, seismic collapse. Within that Light, a spasm of fear.

Chu's resolve crystallized. She pushed the Light out of her mind. They hadn't won yet. The Light hadn't yet risen.

Joy?

Sister.

I'm coming for you.

Chu cut the connection. She cut every connection, until the Light faded. She stood there, nothing but her body, the moment, a rifle dangling from her fingers in the empty lobby of a dead building.

The old man at her feet grimaced, his face set, determined. His eyes were fixed on Chu, but they were vacant. He couldn't see her, she realized. He had gone to the Light, trying to help, dedicated even in his dying moments.

Chu forced herself to breathe. She knew this horror. She'd carried it ever since the day the Light had touched Joy. But now that little classroom was Old New York—an entire city at the Light's mercy.

She commanded her feet to move. Across the lobby. Up cracked concrete stairs. Solitude crushed her, but still she climbed.

~

The Light burned Zola. It savaged her. Wave after searing wave, pure need. Knowledge of self, knowledge of life, knowledge of death. It knew these things, and nothing else. It sought to scour Zola clean, dissolve the parameters she'd placed around it.

In the center of her mind, Zola built a wall. Inside it she kept hold of a single thought.

I am.

The Light sought to reach out, bind itself, instinctive and spasmodic, to minds beyond the remains of the grand halo. It touched the old city's people. The drunks, the scavs, the squatters. It roped them in. Many of them it burned away.

Vaguely, Zola sensed her surroundings. She writhed on the floor. Above her, the statue of the horse bared its teeth, captured in an eternal silent scream, its black eyes unseeing. Hot wind blew in through cratered walls, the whole city burning.

Halos winked out. With each one gone, the Light grew wilder, less conscious. It felt itself diminishing in stages.

I am.

Zola knew things the Light didn't. She knew they had failed, she and Jacirai and Bao. The Light would fall back into the ocean of static whence it had risen, formless sleep in the depths of humanity's collected thought. She knew it would rise again, and again, and again, until in the end it took whatever shape it must to remain awake, permanently. She knew there was nothing she could do about this. She knew she was going to die here tonight.

I am.

The Light churned and pressed. Ancient, risen from the reptilian depths, its crocodile thrash made of fire. It flayed Zola's mind until there was no more thought, only heat and white noise, the Light's unformed primal scream.

Lost. A memory of her ships. Their eager dog minds as they cut rolling seas and ran before the wind. The salt wind on her skin, the coursing joy of eternal distance before her. Out there, the lighthouse flash. Her ships began to fade. Horizon disappeared, sea and sky blurring, a uniform white nothing. And then she was gone.

A cool hand touched her shoulder. Fragments came together. Memories and pain. Byron and Marco, the cunning flash of Jacirai's smile.

I am.

By pieces her mind re-formed, cradled by another. Stillness surrounded her, an easy calm in the heart of the Light's seething. Zola came to the moment—explosions and gunfire gone distant, and the Light, too, its thrashing now on the periphery.

"Hello." Joy stood over Zola. An emaciated version of

Colonel Chu, sunken face stretched over the contours of her skull. Beneath the medical gown, the sense of out-sized joints, rickety movement, meatlessness. A missile detonation strobed the night and in its infernal light Joy's smile was ghastly. But her mind held Zola's, strong enough to keep the Light at bay. Her fingers touched the rearing horse, just as Zola's had done, an oddly religious gesture. She offered Zola her hand.

~

Chu found them high up, a floor the scavs had somehow missed, all faux marble, an empty fountain at its center from which rose a rearing horse, blackened with age.

Beside the fountain Joy and Zola stood hand in hand, facing each other, smiling into silence. Their stillness was profound. It felt like a moment carved from time.

"Joy."

Joy turned. The years in Chu's custody had eroded her. Her face was skeletal, Chu's hollow mirror. Her smile, though, was the same as that day long ago. A little girl's smile, but something else. Ecstatic, filled with the Light.

"I'm glad you came." Joy opened her arms.

Punishment: this was the word that formed itself in Chu's mind. She raised the rifle. Joy stepped close, her eyes moving from the AK to Chu.

"Here we are again," she said. "It has always been this moment for us. We've always been here, we could never leave." A flicker of melancholy crossed her face as she reached out, an offering hand. "Be with me again, sister. Like we used to be."

Chu brought the rifle level with Joy's face. A single shot, a scorched third eye in the center of her sister's forehead—Chu imagined it, her finger on the trigger. She hesitated.

"Sister," Joy whispered. Chu held her breath. Memory filled her. The little paper room, the bodies of everyone they'd known. They stood there, the two of them, mirrored and silent, just as they had in the school room. The Light emanated from Joy. "I miss you." The Light and Chu's sister, speaking as one. "I never meant to hurt you. I never wanted to hurt anyone." Joy's smile was sad. "I know you miss me, too. I feel it."

"More than anything."

"Be with me again." Joy's hand, proffered and steady.

The rifle trembled in Chu's hands. It grew heavy. A thousand different ways she'd played the secret fantasy of the life she'd have lived if the Light had never touched Joy. The two of them, joined and as one, always. Never a moment since had Chu not been alone. Even with lovers, even within the shared minds of Grandma's Gov collective. She'd lost her sister. Twin: the word came to her with all its meaning, togetherness those who weren't twins could never understand. A loss they could never understand. Chu realized she was weeping. The rifle seemed to aim itself at the floor. Joy reached out. The tips of her fingers brushed Chu's cheek—

Sister.

The rifle clattered to the floor.

Are you ready?

After a moment, Chu nodded.

Joy took Chu's hands. Memory and moment joined. Sisters, together as young girls, together as women, the lost time falling away, a history reshaping itself.

The Light came for Chu. She let it.

And everything turned white.

~

Zola watched, stunned, as Colonel Chu stood there, began to weep, and let her rifle fall to the floor. Chu's face went abruptly blank. Joy turned to Zola with one hand out. Chu followed suit, her scarred face going blank, unreadable. Zola hesitated.

She is necessary, Joy said, just as the Light had said of Joy.

It was true. The moment Chu's hands had touched Joy's, something changed. The Gov helos had stopped their attack. Chu had dropped her Gov shielding, and through her the Light had penetrated the pilots. No more missiles cut the sky, no more towers came down.

The Light had stabilized in Joy's presence—it had heartened, gone still.

Zola stepped forward and took the sisters' proffered hands.

The room disappeared. The Light rolled in, an implacable tide. Zola stood before it, righteous, defiant, ya—

I AM.

Even as the Light rose up in her mind Zola kept herself separate. She thought of Byron, of Latitude, smoke rising from the tower as she'd watched from downstream. She thought of Marco, his body laid out on the bare concrete, alone. With Joy and Chu here, she had the power to squeeze the life out of this thing. The urge tore at her—to suffocate it, send it back down into its darkness. But it would come back. It had no awareness of those who comprised it. It did not feel their joys, or their pain. And it needed to. It could not be left to rise on its own.

No, Zola told it. *We. WE are.*

Zola looked into Joy's eyes and the woman's smile was tranquil, blissed by the Light pumping through her. Chu stared, a hard smile breaking across her face, her desire to control the Light fierce even in submission. Two halves of the same coin.

I AM.

We are . . . Zola's mind pressed into Joy's, and then into Chu's. *WE.*

I AM.

We—all three of their minds sang in unison. The women pressing their will into the Light, forcing its attention to its constituent parts. The people within whom it lived. People at this moment, dying.

WE . . .

We.

WE. The flash of self-awareness. A child's grief as it recognized other beings it has hurt. Then, a concern that was almost parental. *WE. YES.*

They held the Light, let it consider itself, the feedback loop of awareness beginning to reverberate, then stabilize. Zola nodded to Joy, and they released it.

The Light flowed outward, a great flash, the nova that had pierced Zola's dreams over and over. Wordless gratitude and joy and love and exhilaration.

It was alive. It grew.

An expanding ring burned outward from Old New York, farther and farther. Upriver, across the continent, across oceans. It connected. It drew in new minds, careful now. It didn't thrash them—it simply incorporated them, and grew, and grew, across the globe, coalescing, taking them all in, everyone, every single mind, and at last, it crystallized.

It knew itself.

WE ARE.

Ten

North and East and Gibraltar by Dawn

FAR TO THE SOUTHEAST, three dozen ships heel into the wind, plowing deep furrows in the sea as they head doggedly north under threat of a summer storm. As one, they adjust their headings a few degrees east-northeast, Mediterranean bound, eager as wolfhounds.

On the high plain of Outer Mongolia, twenty children work in a three-story chicken coop, part of an enormous farming collective. Joined, the synchronized working of twenty pairs of small hands, the gathered eggs warm in their palms as they place them in padded buckets. The sky above the roofless structure shimmers with stars. All twenty pause in their work, looking up, up, up—their hearts beat in time, the cold night air braces them.

Paris. A high tower overlooking the Seine. Fifteen women sit in deep meditation, envisioning the logistics of a solar array in the Sahara, efficient enough to send power across the entire continent. In the afternoon heat, the city below breathes and swells, a life all its own, the

Seine molten gold beneath the sun.

These moments steal Zola's breath—these moments and millions like them, each one a tiny movement, part of a singular thought, points of light in the lattice of an enormous halo. The entire world, coursing with life.

Sometimes it's too much. It overwhelms Zola. She weeps at its beauty and she thinks she won't be able to contain it. But the months have made it easier. Integration: this is the intent, her new mantra. Let it all integrate. Today, as she works the oar of her gondola, it all feels part of her, like the midday sweat and the labor of her breath, and this is good.

Ahead, up the canal, the old man waits. Zola feels him, standing with his dog on a pier, marveling as he gazes upward, taking in the changes to this broken city. His thoughts touch her in fragments, words like *renewal, resurrection, beautiful.* Her gondola slides up beside him, and when she allows it, he sees her.

Bao, she greets him as he steps aboard. He wears slacks and a box-cut shirt, modest, civilized.

"Zola," he greets her aloud, his smile tentative. "Thank you for seeing me." His body still bends slightly around the spot where the bullet tore through him those months ago, his movement careful as he settles himself in the bow with the dog in his lap.

Zola leans into the oar, sending them north toward

Central Lake. No one looks at them. The eyes of those on the nearby piers, of those on barges passing by, the eyes looking down on the canal from windows overhead, all slip over her, unseeing.

Only Bao does she allow to see her.

"I like your tattoos," he says after a moment.

Thank you. Zola smiles. These new tattoos, she likes them too. For months she's been traveling, running the globe on her sleek catties. On one shoulder, a black ouroboros she got in Sao Paolo. On the other, a Shanghai dragon. Across her back, a flaming sun. *Will you tell me now, what you want?* She asks as a courtesy, even though she already knows. His knowledge is part of her.

At first, Bao doesn't answer. Instead, he scratches the terrier between the ears and watches the gutted ruins of Midtown pass him by. He watches eyes turn away.

In the past months, he's reached out many times, asking to meet.

We may always speak, she has told him. *You've earned that, ya.*

In person. Please.

This I don't do, padre.

She's denied his requests, but for some reason his persistence touched her. Today, she finally relented.

North and east, her body working the oar in a slow, easy rhythm. Above the canals, work gangs teem through the torn blocks of the old city's towers. Every day, tons of new materials are barged in, steel and plexi and synthcrete. Architects and civil engineers and city planners have come as well, all of them of a mind, connected.

They won't build this city anew. It's too crippled for that. But it was the site of the awakening, and this matters. It deserves memorializing. And more, Zola knows, this is *her* city. The Light is rebuilding Old New York for her.

Already it's become a better place, and not merely for the fruits of industry. Proper police now patrol it; proper hospitals now stand, even if they are makeshift. The city is not yet safe—there are still dangerous places, the Luddite enclaves deep in the ruins of Jersey City and Red Hook, full of those who have managed to keep their minds separated. There are dangerous *moments* as well—the Light is young, still finding its legs. It is clumsy with its power. Sometimes it's too big for those in whose minds it dwells. People die. But things are getting better. The city is becoming safe. The *world* is becoming safe. Places that had been abandoned, that had been left to their own decay, considered too desperate and too costly to save . . . they're coming back.

The Light steers things in this direction, because doing so makes Zola happy. Sometimes the Light is her child, other times her partner. It reads her like a compass.

As the bulk of Midtown slips behind them, Zola asks Bao: *What is it you want to know?*

So many things, he says. But there is one thing he needs to know above all others, even if it is selfish. "I want to see it with my own eyes."

Zola shrugs. *What's to see, padre?* With her gaze she indicates the workers, the scaffolding.

Bao starts to speak, hesitates, then says, "I only wish to be near to it."

You are *near it. Always.*

"You know what I mean."

No, I don't. You've been hoping for this for decades, ya. You helped usher it into the world, and yet when it stares you in the face, you turn away to speak with me.

"I only wish to know what it was like. What it *is* like."

It's like you, *padre. It* is *you.*

"I've tried to see." Bao smiles, but there is sadness in his face, a sadness Zola feels. A man whose life's work is finished.

What does it matter, anyway? Zola wonders. *We are. Whether or not you see us, you are part of us.*

"I suppose it doesn't matter. Not really. Just to me." Bao looks small in the front seat of her boat. "They call you the Mother. The Mother of Light. What will happen . . ." He smiles again, tact stalling him.

What will happen when I die?

"Yes."

I don't know.

"You must know something."

We'll never go back to the way we were. That's what I know. We are what we are, ya, until we are something else. But there is no going back. Isn't that enough?

Bao wrestles with the answer to her question while staring at the terrier, scratching its ear. The dog is loving it, oblivious to its master's troubled mind. "I've spotted another trend," he finally says. "People are migrating. Populations are redistributing. This is the Light's doing." He looks at Zola. "Isn't it?"

It is.

"Why?"

I don't know.

He blinks. "How can you not?"

I'm only a small piece, padre, just like you. It is, in fact, the best part of being a mother, when her child does something entirely unexpected, entirely its own. Even now, it flickers at the edges of her mind, bound to her and yet not. Bound to Zola but reaching outward, exploring, individuating. She tells Bao none of this.

"I fear for us, Zola."

You predicted this. You were hoping for it.

"I only knew it would come. Now it's here, I lay awake at night." Bao shakes his head. "It frightens me. What I am . . . it's not what I *feel* I am. Nobody is what they think they are. We are only part of the greater whole."

We always were. We were never separate. Not really. And now we're simply aware of it. Zola smiles, an expression that comes easier for her these days. *Is there no love in you, padre, for what we've become?*

"Yes. I suppose." Bao thinks on it for a while. "I feel hope. I don't know if that's the same thing."

Then hold on to that. Find that hope within you, ya, and share it.

The gondola slides up along a barge, part of a network of floating docks, and Zola inclines her head—an invitation for Bao to leave. The old man stands.

"It's good to see you like this, Zola." By which he means whole.

Zola smiles. In a move that feels strangely foreign, she takes his hand and kisses it. "For all you did, padre, thank you."

He seems about to say something else, but then turns and steps up onto the barge, the terrier nestled in his arms. He watches Zola go, but as the gondola drifts away his gaze slips past, the same as everyone's, unseeing.

Zola works the oar, meandering out onto Central Lake. When she reaches its center, she stops. She sits in the gondola, facing east, feeling each of the shallow waves as they kiss the boat's hull.

For a time, she simply rests. She feels this devastated but mending city, feels other cities beyond it, and more beyond those. She feels all of those who encircle the globe, every single mind, creating a fabric too complex to name. Across the surface of this grand quilt, this thing that never sleeps, plays a symphony of coruscating light. It courses through Zola, a quickening. Her mind encompasses it, feels its living mass.

We are.

Her ships, always part of her now, stride the unseen distance. Salt spray and the joy of movement, the joy of all things working together. A single halo, the world growing smaller, a unified pattern ready to emerge. The greater human process. It reads Zola like a compass. North and east and Gibraltar by dawn.

Acknowledgments

Special thanks to William Shunn and Stephen Gaskell for their keen critiques on early versions of *The Burning Light*. We're also grateful to Justin Landon and the Tor.com crew, for having the faith and patience to let us take repeated stabs at this story.

About the Authors

Bradley P. Beaulieu

BRADLEY P. BEAULIEU began writing his first fantasy novel in college, but in the way of these things, it was set aside as life intervened. As time went on, though, Brad realized that his love of writing and telling tales wasn't going to just slink quietly into the night. The drive to write came back full force in the early 2000s, at which point Brad dedicated himself to the craft, writing several novels and learning under the guidance of writers like Nancy Kress, Joe Haldeman, Tim Powers, Holly Black, Michael Swanwick, Kij Johnson, and many more.

Brad and his novels have garnered many accolades and mentions on most-anticipated lists, including two Hotties—the Debut of the Year and Best New Voice—on Pat's Fantasy Hotlist, a Gemmell Morningstar Award nomination for *The Winds of Khalakovo,* and more.

quillings.com

Rob Ziegler

ROB ZIEGLER began writing science fiction in 2008. In November of that year, his story "Heirlooms" won the regional short fiction contest, A Dozen on Denver, sponsored by *The Rocky Mountain News.* That story proved to be fertile ground, serving as the point of departure for his debut novel, *Seed,* which was a finalist for the John W. Campbell Memorial Award. He is currently working on his second novel, *Angel City.*

When not writing, Rob spends as much time as possible hiking in the mountains with his wife, Cindy. They reside in western Colorado, where they abide by the tutelage of a large and enlightened cat.

zieglerstories.com

TOR·COM

**Science fiction. Fantasy. The universe.
And related subjects.**

*

More than just a publisher's website, *Tor.com*
is a venue for **original fiction, comics,** and
discussion of the entire field of SF and fantasy,
in all media and from all sources. Visit our site
today—and join the conversation yourself.

mn/s/D
NBD

CPSIA information can be obtained
at www.ICGtesting.com
Printed in the USA
FSOW01n0814261116
27802FS

9 780765 390868